YELL, SAM, IF YOU STILL CAN

D1344721

Only one Marguerite in the yard. This is for her.

YELL, SAM, IF YOU STILL CAN

LE TIERS TEMPS

MAYLIS BESSERIE
TRANSLATED BY CLÍONA NÍ RÍORDÁIN

THE LILLIPUT PRESS
DUBLIN

First published in English in 2022 by
THE LILLIPUT PRESS
62–63 Sitric Road, Arbour Hill
Dublin 7, Ireland
www.lilliputpress.ie

First edition, *Le Tiers Temps* © Editions GALLIMARD, Paris, 2020

Paperback ISBN 9781843518341

10 9 8 7 6 5 4 3 2 1

The Lilliput Press gratefully acknowledges the financial
support of the Arts Council/An Chomhairle Ealaíon.

Set in 10.25pt on 16.5pt Le Monde Livre by iota (www.iota-books.ie)
Printed in Kerry by Walsh Colour Print

ACT ONE

Le Tiers-Temps, Residence for Senior Citizens, Paris
25 July 1989

She is dead. I have to remind myself constantly – Suzanne is not in the bedroom. She is not with me. She is no longer present. She is … buried. Yet, this morning, when I was under my old blankets, it felt as if she were here, buried under the blankets with me, and not dead. Here, huddled up against her old Sam. As a matter of fact, it is only because she is here, leaning against my old bones, stretched lengthways against my carcass, that I know that I'm not underground myself.

I'm a little cold all the same. I'm all skin and bone. My mother was forever telling me that. When I was a child, I ran all the time, in the streets, in the fields. I ran to keep myself warm because I was skin and bone. I ran so that I didn't have to listen to May telling me that I was all skin and bone. I ran. One day, I ran for such a long time that I really ran away. Ran off and escaped over sea. Ran far away from May.

Suzanne ran alongside me for a long time. Through the forest, on the dead wet leaves, over the roots buried deep beneath the trees. We ran with the wind at our backs, pushing us further and further into the night. We were afraid of our feet rustling in the leaves under our weight. So, we ran ever faster, we ran scared. Suzanne's feet hurt but she ran all the same. The brambles pricked us. My feet beat against the ground, I could feel my heart racing, like Suzanne's. Suzanne was clutching at my shoulders, at my overcoat, she was hanging on to me, wanting me to lift her feet that were weary from the weight of the earth. The earth was like a load she was carrying, like lead, so heavy it would split your soles.

I couldn't feel my feet any more. I ran for me and for Suzanne. One foot for each of us. Lifting them out of fear. She had pulled me along for so long, she was exhausted, dead on her feet. Suzanne is dead. She is not in the bedroom. She has let go of my overcoat. Suzanne has left me.

I'm cold under the blankets. Today is Friday, I think. The only thing I can see from my bed is a plucked plane tree. In Dublin, I could hear the gulls' cries. The city belongs to them and they hoot and squawk – at every door. They surround the towers in Sandycove and fly in flocks right into the centre of town. Squealing. Eating everything they find. They're a sight to behold, like predators on the prowl. I can see myself in Ireland, picking up the pace. My swift shadow reflected in the Liffey, the gulls snapping at my heels. I thought the noise was my knees knocking together, but it was only the sound of my soles clacking on the grey stones. Later, when I used to come to see May (to see my mother), the gulls had grown fatter again. They knocked off the leftovers from the boats

4

travelling on the Liffey. They guzzled the leftovers left in the bins – they stole from the poor; they ate the leftovers and even the poor themselves.

On Rue Dumoncel, I cannot hear the gulls. I cannot even hear Suzanne. I cannot hear anything any more. I can only hear what I have already heard.

I'm cold under the blankets. I need to think of a song.

> Bid adieu, adieu, adieu,
> Bid adieu to girlish days.

The voice of Joyce. It warms my heart. The voice of Joyce under my old blankets. He makes music even when he writes. His feet flit from one piano pedal to the other. Joyce plays and sings with a Cork accent. His father's accent. He still has quite a good tenor voice. He sings for his friends – the Jolas, the Gilberts, the Léons; he sings for Nino. I'm under the table, under the weather, listening to him. The house shakes, a girl dances. Joyce's daughter, Lucia. I close my eyes. When Joyce stops the show, he gets up on his three feet – his own feet and his walking stick. He bows and then, at once, asks for a drink. He is Irish.

I used to drink in Grogan's, on South William Street. I would meet my friend Geoffrey there, Geoffrey Thompson. He was always flanked by a number of acolytes leaning on the counter. I would meet him and we would have a drink together. In winter, I can remember customers leaning on the counter, like sparrows on a wire. They used to put their caps and hats down next to their drinks to make themselves comfortable. I like Grogan's. The wooden floors and panelling, the rays of blue and orange light when the sun shines through the stained-glass windows. I remember that all of the customers would be dressed the same – white shirts, buttoned waistcoats, black jackets and shoes. Geoffrey had a moustache. A thick moustache that dripped when he drank. In the pub, he used to have his happy evening air. Geoffrey is good company. In Ireland, men crack jokes without daring to look each other in the eye. They are funny and shy. They are funny but the humour doesn't reach their eyes. They look into the distance when they tell a joke. They stare at the clean glasses on the shelves, or at the pint glasses, stained with traces of foam. In Dublin, everything is intimidating and everything is banned. I left, ran away.

MEDICAL FILE
File number: 835689

Mr Samuel Barclay Beckett
Age: 83
Height: 1.82m (6 feet)
Weight: 63 kg (9.9 stone)

Section 1

The patient is an 83-year-old writer, referred by his friend, Dr Sergent, for emphysema and multiple falls resulting in losses of consciousness.

There is a history of Parkinson's disease on Mr Beckett's maternal side.

On 27 July 1988, his wife found him unconscious on the kitchen floor. He was admitted to the hospital in Courbevoie, where tests showed no evidence of fractures and no internal bleeding. He was subsequently transferred to the Hôpital Pasteur in order to investigate the cause of his falls.

At present, he displays none of the three classic symptoms of Parkinson's disease: resting tremor, bradykinesia (akinesia), extrapyramidal rigidity. However, the typical motor symptoms (muscular rigidity and postural instability) have led the neurological team at the hospital to suspect that he may be suffering from an atypical or associated form of the disease.

The patient also says that he finds it increasingly difficult to write (dysgraphia) and to hold his pen.

In light of his 'fragile' physical state, it was recommended that he should move into a medicalized retirement home.

He has been living in Le Tiers-Temps retirement home since 3 August 1988. His wife has since died. He was seriously malnourished on arrival. The high-calorie diet, parenteral nutrition and high-flow oxygen therapy have improved his state. He has been allowed out of the residence for solo walks in dry weather, when he feels able to do so.

NURSING NOTES ON MR BECKETT

Nadja, nurse:
Mr Beckett adheres strictly to his daily routine. He writes in the evening and gets up late. I usually go into his room at the end of my rounds, at about 9.45 or 10 am, so that I don't disturb him.

He is not on a drip, and can wash and dress himself unaided.

He is a very quiet patient, and is polite to staff.

At his own request, he eats his meals in his room and does not participate in the activities organized for residents.

When he feels capable, he leaves the residence at the beginning of the afternoon to go for a fifteen- to twenty-minute walk, as recommended by his physiotherapist. People come to visit him at the end of the afternoon. He drinks a little alcohol and continues to smoke.

Treatment:
– High-calorie diet administered orally until his weight returns to within normal range.
– Oxygen therapy via face mask, at one to two litres per minute.

Le Tiers-Temps, Residence for Senior Citizens, Paris

26 July 1989

I'm in the garden. I'm not sure if it can really be called a garden, but I'm 'in the garden'. That's what they call it here. I'll use its given name. In the garden, the lawn is made out of green, non-slip plastic. It's a fake lawn and you walk on it as if it were real, and yet it's not because you can't lie down on it. And that's how I come to be in the garden.

I'm not very steady on my feet this morning. The man who comes every morning to get me to exercise my legs said: 'Mr Beckett, you're not very steady on your feet this morning.' I did my exercises all the same. I did them as best I could. I raised my leg and set it down again. I did it again and again, as often as he asked. I did the same with the other one. With the other one, it's a bit harder. I lift it, or at least I try to: I grit my teeth, but my leg doesn't co-operate. I lift it all the same and I set it down again. I fail and I try again. All the same,

I manage to walk. Well, walk is a bit of an exaggeration. I push one leg, and move it, so it ends up a couple of centimetres in front of the other. My feet move at a snail's pace and work at walking, but they're not working that well.

There's a strip of fake grass next to the wall. A strip of lawn. That's where I walk, when I'm not very steady. Some days, Nadja, the nurse, walks on the strip of lawn with me. Her hair is shiny; she must put some sort of perfumed hair oil on it. I can smell the oil when she takes my arm, as if I were her elderly husband. I can feel her as she brushes against my old carcass to help it move. I can feel her. What does she think when she takes my motionless arm and I look at her from behind my thick owl glasses? I don't know. She's doing her job. She's kind. If I bore her she gives nothing away. I can smell her hair from a distance. I don't go up to her – I'm ashamed of what she might feel. I keep my arm by my side, hoping she'll take it. It doesn't happen every day.

The wall that surrounds the garden is high. At the E.N.S. on Rue d'Ulm, there were no walls, but the railings were high. I had to climb over the railings. I hopped over them to go drinking. I drank and hopped over the railings. I hopped over and back. On the way out and on the way home. It was a less elegant hop on the way back but it was a hop all the same. I drank with my old friend Tom. Never before 5 pm. Absolutely never. At the Cochon de Lait I drank Mandarin curaçaos, Fernet-Brancas and Real-Ports. I was drunk as a lord. Even lost my glasses, stumbled and tripped, gabbing – like a hermit breaking his vow of eternal silence. A drunken idiot, a cheerful drunk. My spirit lightened by my heavy load. Light, so light-hearted. Had I only listened to my father,

I could have spent happy days at Guinness's, that radiant, flourishing brewery. Happy and hoppy. Alas, the memories come flooding back now that I'm finished. Now that I no longer know how to write. That I no longer write. Almost not at all.

I used to drink with Joyce too. In gorgeous glasses. We'd drink at nightfall, when the beasts return to the byre, huge quantities of white Fendant de Sion. Joyce converted everyone to his tipple – which reminded him of the urine of an archduchess, he used to say. Joyce converted everyone. Joyce was a real archduchess.

If anyone thinks that I amn't divine
He'll get no free drinks when I'm making the wine.
But I have to drink water and wish it were plain
That I make when the wine becomes water again.

Good God, this garden stinks of piss. Rivers of codgers' piss trickling onto the fake grass. Had it been real, the grass would have turned yellow. Luckily, it's plastic. It keeps its colour. A little rinse and it's gone. But nothing can be done about the stench. Nothing to be done in any case.

In the garden, I'm afraid of being taken. Afraid that someone will say: *Mr Beckett, I'll give you a hand*. And they'll take my arm as if I were an elderly aunt to be promenaded around the garden. To whom they would show the flowers. Or the clouds. I tremble at the thought of being touched. That someone might touch me. I always expect the worst. Once upon a time, though, I was touched often. Peggy, for instance, touched me a lot. She touched me with gusto. She would grab hold of me like a warrior grabs the saddle of his mount before pulling himself upright on top of it. She would harpoon me with her solid hands. She would hang on to my flesh, would pull it off my bones and brandish it like a trophy. She caught hold of me with such enthusiasm. I don't know what it meant. If it was real love. But she sank her hook in me and I liked it. I mean I let her at it. And if I let her at it I must have liked it. Of course. Liked that she hung on to me, burning my bark. Liked that she skinned me like a rabbit whose pyjama pelt is peeled off after being stunned by a heavy stone. Yes, I liked it. I liked it for a long time.

In Foxrock, there was also that girl. Her name escapes me. The girl who liked to pinch me on the train. When I boarded at the station in Glenageary, she was often there on the train. Quite pretty. In an Irish way. She would sit down beside me, a fountain of hair dripping down her back. The fine girl would pinch me with her fearsome fat fingers. The big finger and the thumb would stick into the side of my ribs, digging in with her nails. I would whinny. And that really made her laugh. I don't remember the beginning of the story. How did she get into the habit of pinching me? I don't know. I must have said something. Something obscene. I'd do that sometimes with strangers – I mean with women I didn't know. I'd say obscene things and sometimes I'd be caught and even pinched. She had a devilishly good time by my side. I had such pleasure between her thighs. I pinched her and she pinched me. Peggy pinched me too. And in the end, it hurt.

PATIENT CARE LOGBOOK

26 July 1989

Sylvie, nurse's aide (9 am–6 pm):

Up at 9.45 am. Had a cup of tea and two slices of toast for breakfast.

Washed and dressed himself.

Physiotherapy from 10 am to 10.20 am.

Had lunch in his room at 11.50 am:

– Mushroom soup

– Filet of cod with lemon, carrot purée

– Stewed blackcurrants

Ate very little. Meals augmented by high-calorie cream desserts to replace the fruit juice the patient dislikes.

Walked as far as Place d'Alésia, was out of breath on his return.

His friend Madame Fournier came to visit. Two glasses of whiskey at around 5 pm.

Nadja, nurse (6 pm–12 pm):

In high spirits at the end of the afternoon. Making joke

Dined in his room at 6.45 pm:

- Potage Polignac
- Pasta salad with ham and mushrooms
- Cream cheese with herbs
- Fruits of the forest pudding

Still at his desk at midnight when my shift finished.

Le Tiers-Temps, Residence for Senior Citizens, Paris

29 July 1989

I am in my room. Décor: bed, bedside locker, commode, book-shelves, mini-fridge supplied by my faithful Edith, my faithful friend. Translator beyond compare.

In front of the window, a table to write at and a cream-coloured telephone. That's about all. The décor would have pleased my mother. It's as gay as her own bedroom – fancy as a Protestant fantasy. This room is not really my room. This is where I am being minded. It's where I reside and where, henceforth, I receive my post. My bed is overhung by a three-bulb light fixture suspended from the ceiling by a chain. Every time there is any movement in the upstairs rooms, it shakes and threatens to give way. Were it to do so, that would be the end. I should be so lucky! It would come crashing down and finish me off. A quick end. A happy accident. Unlikely. Not every day is filled with adventure. A couple of lines in the paper: *Lighting strikes! Never before was an Irishman* (he was only a shadow of himself) *hammered like that.* For the moment, the light is still there, hanging over my soft brain.

When I turn on the light, at around 6 pm, my room turns wild. I mean the colour. It suits the wallpaper. It sets it free. The dirty yellow becomes almost mauve or muddy brown. When I am seated at my table at around 6 pm, I gaze at the moon if the sky is cloudless. Night falls on me, as if I were by the lake in Glendalough. My father ruffles my hedgehog hair, in silence. Night falls, in silence. We look at it fall and we wait. We wait a little longer, as the light fades. *That's it*, says my father. That's it; it's almost at an end. The pink clouds are going to disappear behind the Wicklow mountains. It's time to go home. To come down. The darkness has altered the paths. My father wraps his belt around my hand and guides me. We are two blind men in a forest. I allow myself to be pulled along by the belt. I lift my legs so I don't stumble over the roots. The dark night links me to my father, in silence. My father is an owl in the night and the moon is all he needs.

When we return, May is raging. Frothing at the mouth. Fuming. She is always furious when she is worried. A few minutes before that, before nightfall at the edge of the lake in Glendalough, before the moon sets, May falls silent. A happy silence. The calm before the storm.

This evening the moon is reddish. My leg hurts; I lean over my table to look at the russet moon. The honey moon. I am in Joyce's room.

'Wait till the honeying of the lune, love!'

I am sitting across from him. A bandage covers his left eye, under his glasses. His thick round glasses. I look at him without knowing if he can see me. The elastic part of the bandage parts his hair above his temples. He stares into the distance. Perhaps at the moon. The honey moon. He is wearing an old-fashioned suit and a striped shirt with mother-of-pearl buttons. The moustache suits him. It was a good idea. It hides his lips, like the peak on a gendarme's cap. A single line of hair connects his mouth to the base of his chin. He dictates all in one go. He crosses his legs, one under the other. I look at him and I do the same. He dictates. I don't know if he can see me. His sight is failing and he lowers his eyes. Perhaps he can just about make out my shadow as he dictates.

We are sitting like two companions in front of the scant pages. I type. The words appear. I type quickly. There is a knock at the door. *Entrez*. Lucia, his much-loved daughter says hello to me. She gives a message to her father and smiles skittishly at me. She is beautiful despite her eyes. She has a squint; the alignment of her eyes is not parallel. I'm not sure if you can use the word *parallel* or *not parallel* when talking about the alignment of eyes. In any case, Lucia's eyes are not parallel. She's still beautiful though.

Lucia leaves Joyce's room. I type Joyce's book, his *Work in Progress* – it progresses slowly. Music of the language, of languages. I type his English that is full of Ireland. He spits out page after page, the Ireland of our mothers. The Ireland of May. It comes to life under my fingers. It's very contagious. Transmitted by the tongue. I took a long time to be cured of it. Of Ireland, of Joyce, of May. Of Joyce, of my mother, of my tongue. Am I cured? I don't know. There's no denying that we are sentenced at birth – to be the sons of our fathers and mothers. To be born of them. Born of May. Far beneath Joyce.

You could say that it started badly. I'm not saying that I did what it takes. No. I could certainly have done better. Taken some precautions. Or even draconian measures. Fighting evil with evil. I could have killed May, for example. Killing my mother would not have been that hard. I had a thousand opportunities to do so. All I needed was a small cushion. Hold it firmly. In silence. Just for a few minutes. May wouldn't have suffered. Or not for long. I could have spared her such a long existence. If you think about it, it wouldn't have been as bad as it sounds. Even for her. A happy escape.

May was a nurse. I could have taken advantage of a moment's fatigue on the way back from a night shift in the wee small hours. I could have put an end to her suffering and to mine. No, to have done things properly I would have had to have killed her before my birth. Or in childbirth, giving birth to me, why not? That would have been ideal. A lucky birth – night and day. Of course, the best solution of all would have been if my grandmother hadn't been born either. We would all have been nipped in the bud. That would have been the simplest solution. But chronologically, I admit, it's a fucking mess.

I don't hold it against her. I don't hold it against her for dragging it out. For hanging on to life, like a limpet clinging to the rocks. She couldn't have known. As a matter of fact, I have held on too. I have wandered Dublin Bay amidst the seaweed and the seals. Yes, the cold sea of Ireland is full of seals. The sea is icy. The seals are the only ones who enjoy themselves. They grow and multiply like loaves, by the grace of God. Fucking like sea rabbits. Lying on the rocks ready to receive the recognition of their peers. The seals, in French *phoques*. A delightful word, if ever there was one. I have never got used to it. A delight. It's all in the ear – when people say *phoque*, I hear fuck. There's no difference, almost none. The way fuck is said in the region that I'm from, with a narrow *u* sound, closed in on itself, almost shamefully, that pronunciation of fuck resembles the fattest ever sea mammal. When it's said like that, you don't sound very keen. Nonetheless, in my memory, my distant memory, it wasn't bad. Not always great, of course. But oftentimes I gave myself wholeheartedly to the exercise of 'fucking'. An exercise that I classified amongst my favourite pastimes – along with cricket and cycling, of course. It went some way to alleviate the punishment of existence. In actual fact, I received very few complaints about the quality of my services. I almost always gave satisfaction – at least on the job. Poor randy old bugger. I'd be better off going to bed and putting an end to writing and thinking. In actual fact, I don't write any more. I rephrase things. I rearrange them. I reorganize them. I have fun with Hiberno-English or with French, depending on my mood. Somersaults is what I do, in what remains. For example, my newest work, or rather my last one, *Stirrings Still*. I say to myself, 'hmm, that wouldn't be bad in French' – like a schoolboy with his Latin homework. I do somersaults with my tongue; that's all I have left. I don't write, I scratch away. I beat my retreat. When did I last write? I don't know. I reply to letters, as I was brought up to do. I reply revealing what's left of my poor life. I send news to my old friends, to my English publishers; they're happy that old Sam sends news, that he continues to scribble away. *There is something left,* they say to themselves. So little is left. Spaces, blanks – the space between. I have so few words left. They have all been worn away, down to the quick. You wouldn't think it but words too can get worn out. Like the seat of your pants. Like the heart. How many words do I really have left? I don't know. A couple of needles left in a haystack. Haystacks again. The same words again, which pirouette and disappear. Today, I have the impression that the page is huge. And that my pen too is limping along. The work of old age. It contaminates everything. Even my letters. My writing is cursive, brief, telegraph-like.

Dear friend, thank you for your letter – stop – Affectionately yours.

Oh, isn't the Nobel laureate long-winded! What rubbish! I'd be better off going to bed and switching off the light. If I fall asleep perhaps I'll find myself in Ireland's freezing seas – an energizing swim, a rejuvenating treatment. I'll open my eyes in the water. I'll allow the salt to turn them red. There might even be mermaids, who knows? I'll dream of seals, *phoques*.

ASSESSMENT OF MR BECKETT'S INDEPENDENCE

30 July 1989

Mr Beckett can make the transfers 'stands up, sits, lies down' (without any material assistance, leaning on the furniture in his vicinity: armrest, bed, table):
- unprompted, without reminders, explanations or needing to be shown what to do;
- he can get up and down to and from bed;
- without putting himself in danger;
- every time this is necessary and required.

He can move around the various living spaces in the residence (common rooms, restaurant, care rooms ...):
- without having to be guided;
- in all spaces right up to the door that gives onto the street;
- in an adequate fashion as befits his capacities;
- whenever he needs and wants to move.

He does not remain within the confines of the residence and regularly goes outside the residence:
- without having to be told what to do;
- until his return to the residence;

- paying appropriate care outside and with a manner befitting his capabilities;
- whenever he feels able to do so.

K.L., psychologist

Le Tiers-Temps, Residence for Senior Citizens, Paris
30 July 1989

My brain is like mush, I've got the shakes. Spreading my spider-like scribbles on paper in my hang-out for almost-down-and-outs. I'm rewriting my own words. Translating myself. Incurable linguistic schizophrenia. Love–hate for the mother tongue. Impossible to unscramble.

I bring together the remaining working cells of my dwindling mind. Laborious work – two lines, no more, on good days. I move forward so slowly that I feel I have almost stopped. In any case, according to the rules of physics, as I continue to slow down it is probable that I will stop. That I will finish with words or they with me.

When Joyce's eyes gave up on him, he found others. He had eyes everywhere. Eyes at his service, blinking at the ready. The eyes of his slaves, the eyes of his angels. I started to work behind my bicycle-wheel glasses. I held his hand, without seeming to, I helped him across, without seeming to. I was at his beck and call, every day at 2 Square de Robiac. When the sky was heavy and the clouds were pink. When it was time to type. We spoke of cows and Ireland.

I can see him still. He crosses his legs. He sticks one of them up on the armrest of the armchair. It dangles. He thinks. The work progresses. His hands are crossed on his knees. My hands and my eyes are at his service, in the service of the work that is progressing.

On Sundays it's another story. My legs still carry me as far as 2 Square de Robiac, to the black door framed with laurel leaves. Joyce doesn't say Sam, he says *Monsieur*. I say *Monsieur* too. Sometimes on Sunday, in front of the door of 2 Square de Robiac, as we are about to turn onto Rue de Grenelle, then Avenue Bosquet heading down to the Seine, he says Beckett. Just Beckett, no *Monsieur*, nothing, with no ceremony.

On the banks of the Seine, it often smells of dog. Dozens of dogs throw themselves joyfully into the water and make a show of themselves. They come out drenched. Their dripping fur gives them a woebegone look. The children stare at them in silence until they shake themselves and then they start to shout. The shower of water from the dogs marks the end of the bathing session. Women in aprons tie the leashes to their collars again. Then it is the turn of the children to paddle in the water, half-naked. If it is warm. If the weather is nice. The dogs' fur dries quickly. On some days, on the banks of the Seine, you can also come across dog-groomers. Straw-hatted with a dog between their legs, held down against their aprons. The wind blows the clumps of hair along the cobblestones.

The dog escapes in the end, with his tail between his legs. There'll be none of that on Sundays.

On Sunday, with the penman on my left, I wander the cobblestoned quays as far as the Île aux Cygnes. This island, which is not one, has a history that is far from banal. A trivial, mythological history. A history like those Joyce loved. Before being connected to the land by order of the sovereign, the island was called Maquerelle. Peasants had their cows graze there. There was never any mackerel, nor even pimps (the French word for pimp is *maquerelle*); the word comes from *ma querelle*, my quarrel. It was a place where quarrels were resolved, with the Seine as a witness, hiding in its depths the weighted-down bodies of the victims and the vanquished. The Liffey too is freighted with these shameful, useless dead, hidden under floods of holy water. Seaside cemeteries of drowned sinners, the suicidal, the betrayed, those who sink in the night into the murky depths. Unsolved crimes, mucky secrets.

It was ever so. People went to fight on the island as needed, discreetly, without bothering anyone else. And then one day the King of France and Navarre was given the gift of swans by an ambassador. Forty swans. Swans which, easier on the eye than the cows, or the peasants and their quarrels, became the lords of the island. His Majesty did everything in his power to protect them. He forbade anyone from entering the island without prior permission, forbade the boatmen from landing there, from taking the eggs or hunting. No matter, the swans soon were no more. The weary swans died out. No doubt after some more quarrels. No one knows. In any case the island still exists. We walked along its banks in almost

26

complete silence. All that was to be heard was the clicking of some fishing rods and the dumb murmur of the eternal admiration that I had, poor dog that I was, for my master.

RULES OF THE RETIREMENT HOME
an extract

Trips outside

Residents can come and go as they please provided they respect the rules put in place to ensure their protection. The establishment is a place of residence. Living within its walls does not mean that residents' freedom should be affected, no matter the state of their health.

When a resident's psychological state allows them to choose their outings, and once they are conscious of the risks being taken, the management will not oppose these outings, no matter the physical risks involved. The psychological state of the residents is assessed by the doctor who decides along with the rest of the team the circumstances under which each resident is allowed outside.

The management cannot be held responsible for the consequences of the residents' outings. A resident leaving the building must alert a member of staff in order to prevent any disruption and to enable the staff rota to be organized accordingly. Should staff not be informed, management will search for the person as soon as they become aware of their absence and will alert family and guardians of the situation.

Le Tiers-Temps, Residence for Senior Citizens, Paris

31 July 1989

Two outings a day in fine weather. A little leftover habit. A little happiness. In quiet obstacle-free streets. Choices have to be made – right or left? On the right-hand side or the left-hand side of Rue Rémy-Dumoncel. More hinges on the decision than is apparent at first sight. For example, imagine that once I leave the guest parlour and go as far as the glass-fronted reception area I decide to turn left – which is what I am about to do. Before going out the door I need to prepare myself to turn. That is one of the distinguishing features of an aged biped, forever condemned to a precarious equilibrium, with only two feet and two arms for hanging onto branches. A fine art. A fine pickle.

On the advice of my physiotherapist, I prepare myself before attempting to swing the weight of my body on the leg known as the *pivoting* leg. I'm clever enough to wait for the door to open so as to hang on to it and swing slightly around. A sensible move, if ever there was one. The attempt is successful.

Once I start off on the left, my stroll along Rue Dumoncel seems easy enough. On this side are the even numbers in decreasing order. Since I have decided to include only quiet streets in my itinerary, I have to rule out continuing my walk on Avenue René-Coty. There are lots of cars and the footpaths are often dug up because of roadworks, making it difficult to get round, and the passers-by are often less than courteous. *Niet*. As luck would have it, at one end of Rue Dumoncel, just before it joins Avenue René-Coty, a junction allows you to turn right (nothing like alternating between right and left) to go up Rue de la Tombe-Issoire. While it is easy to walk down Rue Dumoncel because of a slight incline – at an angle that is just steep enough to allow one to walk comfortably without hurrying – Rue de la Tombe d'Issoire is deceptively flat. I walk along there in any case, breathing in deeply every couple of steps to conserve my energy. Here I am in the street of the giant Issoire who, once upon a time, robbed travellers and whose decapitated head is buried somewhere under my old feet. I have walked so far. On roads and in forests. Crossed over ditches, worn out the soles of my boots. One day, one of my old galoshes exploded on the Boul' Mich. Walking along like a tramp, the maw of my shoe open, sock exposed to the elements, I had no other option but to hurry into the first shop I came across. I acquired a new pair. Pointed elegant Italian shoes. Like the ones Joyce used to wear. New shoes for a fresh start, for take-off. I abandoned my old kicks in the new cardboard box. My winkle-pickers were thick and heavy.

Lightened by the load of their presence and by the memory of the kilometres I had walked in them, I walked. I walked with my new shoes. Place Edmond-Rostand, Rue de Médicis, Rue de Vaugirard. I trotted along like a mad young dog until I reached Rue de Grenelle. Arrived at Square de Robiac. Joyce wasn't home. There was only his daughter to greet me. Lucia served me some tea with a facetious smile. Lucia didn't call me *Monsieur*, or *Beckett*. When we went to the cinema or the theatre, she used to slip her arm through mine and pull me close. Lucia used to call me *Sam. My Sam. My dear Sam.*

I soon stopped walking out with her. I didn't walk out with Lucia for long. I dawdled a bit, it's true, but we didn't walk out together for long. One spring day I told Lucia that I wouldn't walk out with her any more. That I was no longer *her Sam*. A storm brewed on the horizon. For a long time, the storm clouds massed over the Joyces' house. I was no longer *her Sam*, the door of Square de Robiac slammed shut. I clammed up myself. Like an oyster.

ONE-ON-ONE INTERVIEW

31 July 1989

Mr Beckett consented freely to the consultations I had suggested to him on arrival.

I see him for a one-on-one interview for thirty to forty minutes every fortnight, with a view to helping and encouraging him to mix with other people again.

Although he is very pleasant and answers my questions, he continues to be rather withdrawn, and this tendency has become more acute since the death of his wife.

He does not want to take part in activities or entertainment organized by staff or external leaders.

Nevertheless, Mr Beckett benefits from an attentive support circle. Every week he receives letters, phone calls and visits from friends or family members.

This withdrawn attitude is consistent with the social life he led before moving to Le Tiers-Temps, with strong intellectual friendships and a fiercely guarded privacy.

He has also experienced the death of many close friends over the past number of years, and this has increased his solitary tendencies.

However, he does seem to have adapted to life at Le Tiers-Temps. He has even continued his writing activities at his own pace.

Given his history and the trauma that he may have experienced, I feel that it would be unnecessary and detrimental to push him to socialize further, as it might upset the fragile equilibrium that he seems to have found here.

K.L., psychologist

Le Tiers-Temps, Residence for Senior Citizens, Paris
2 August 1989

A broth of Franco-Irish thoughts. Poor old fogey. I'd be better off going to bed. Put down my book. Switch off my lamp. Joyce's lamp. Click. Have I switched it off properly? It's so difficult to hear the click. I'll do it again, just in case. Is the lamp switched off? No one answers. No one will answer, Sam. It appears to be switched off. I put on my glasses and look at my lamp. I switch it on and switch it off again. I switch it on to switch it off. No change. Just the light.

A ray of moonlight lights up the floor and reaches as far as the other side of my bedspread. We might even be down Combray's way: cheeks on the pillow and the chink of light under the door. Any doubts are dissipated. The light, the other one, that comes through the gaps around the door frame comes from the corridor – a privilege reserved for old crocks who have been herded together in one place. The light is left on in the corridor just in case. The shades are chased away. The spectres are lit up. In the night-time, people have been known to die in the light. To burn, like moths to the flame.

Joyce's lamp. After Lucia, the door of the house on Square de Robiac was slammed shut. The light was switched off. Click. Persona non grata. What happened? I don't know any more. I wandered inhospitable cities. I wandered, searching for my words, until the light came back. One day, it did come back. I found the light at the end of the Allée des Cygnes where the penman was waiting for me. Found Joyce, in the end.

Hark, there is talking on the other side. The steps are drawing closer. They're on their rounds. The watchmen are on duty. White coats or blue coats, feet in their clogs. Lights out. Curfew for the old people. Or perhaps it's already daytime. I don't know any more in the dark of my room, the end resembles the beginning. I could also be on my island with May and my father as he is dying. My father lying outstretched on his bed in the house between the sea and the mountain. The smell of sweet pea filling his nostrils. His brave heart gives out. He's swearing now. Swearing that he will soon climb to the top of Howth, lie down in the bracken and fart from the top of the hill. He swears that it's not the end, that he will admire Dublin Bay once more. *Fight, fight and fight*, he says. Then there is silence. How silent and empty everything is. I no longer know what to say. I'm at a loss for words.

There is a knock at the door.

I don't want to speak. I wouldn't know what to say, what to respond.

There is another knock.

I cover my face with my sheets.

'*Monsieur l'Irlandais? Houhou, Monsieur l'Irlandais?*'

Who is that crazy woman bleating at my door? Or am I so far gone that I'm off my rocker? I'll switch on the light. No, if I turn it on, she'll know that I'm awake. I'll switch it off. It's not on, I mean the lamp. The crazy woman is on full alert and is still knocking at the door.

'*Vous êtes là, Monsieur l'Irlandais? Je voulais dire* … GOOD NIGHT!'

I stay under the white cotton sheet, the one with the red border embroidered with Le Tier-Temps's initials, breathing in through the cloth, inhaling the powerful odour of the detergent whose only virtue is its capacity to cover all the other smells. The coot giggles again. A voice calls her.

'Madame Pérouse, what are you doing up and about? I'll bring you back to your room.'

I reach for the oxygen mask the doctor suggested I wear all night. I fumble for it carefully, in the dark. I pull it on and gasp like a man starved of oxygen, a draining-the-oxygen-tank man, someone starved for air. Never mind the lights and lamps. Just air. Coming up for air, goddammit!

PATIENT CARE LOGBOOK

3 August 1989

Thérèse, nurse's aide (midnight–8 am):
The light in Mr Beckett's room was on until 2 am.

I went to see him at around 1 am. I knocked at his door and he answered. He was sitting at his table, reading. I suggested he continue his reading in bed so as to vary his posture and not tire himself out.

He moved unaided from table to bed in my presence.

I allowed him to decide, in an autonomous fashion as he requested, as to when he should switch off his light.

Sylvie, nurse's aide (9 am–6 pm):
Out of bed at 10 am. It was difficult to wake him. Mr Beckett didn't want any breakfast and decided to go back to sleep.

He assured me that he had his own 'provisions' in his fridge and that he could eat later.

Personal hygiene:
Bathed, and assumes his own self-care. Washed his upper body (to include shaving and hair-combing) and lower body (intimate hygiene and lower limbs).

Requested help to cut his toenails.

Dressing:

Mr Beckett chooses his clothes in his wardrobe and gets them ready himself.

The dressing of the upper body (vest, shirt, sweater) and middle-body region (buttons, zips, belts) is carried out with no difficulty.

The dressing of the lower body (socks and shoes) takes him a lot of time.

Le Tiers-Temps, Residence for Senior Citizens, Paris
3 August 1989

I was woken by a phone call from Hermine, Blin the stage director's widow. Since Blin's death she rings me often, even early in the morning. I'm a night owl though, and this is a well-known fact. When he was putting on *Godot*, Roger himself used to say, *Sam is a night owl, Sam is a tomcat*. Roger is dead. I can recall that much. Hermine also re-calls me. Especially since Roger's death. She says, 'I haven't woken you, I hope.' She does know she is waking me. She does it all the same. It doesn't matter.

Dreamed of Lucia. Lucia at the Bal Bullier. The whole family was there. The penman was there with his wife, Nora. They were all there to cheer on their daughter. A costume of fish scales stuck to Lucia's skin. Sparkling emerald-green sequins covered her legs and body, right up to her neck. Bare arms. Her thighs came together in a fishtail. Her hair is plaited with green and silver. She looks at me. She is more beautiful than my memory of her; long-limbed Lucia who dances to Schubert. She dances and she looks at me. Joyce too looks at me. I force myself to look elsewhere. I notice a spotted dog at my feet. I can hear Lucia and Schubert, but I'm looking at the dog. He has two deep-set bad-tempered eyes. The eyes of a savage.

Dance steps – *gargouillade, saut de biche* – I listen to Lucia spinning in the air while my eyes, always busy with other things, study the glass roof. I stare at the blinding overhead light. I listen to Schubert, and to Lucia who glides around on his notes. Perhaps she is crawling. The light burns me and my eyes look away. When they come to rest again on the stage, the stage where Lucia is dancing, the dog bites me. The damned mutt has Joyce's mouth. Ding.

After waking, I took a bath without assistance from the nurse – this is rare enough to be noteworthy. I don't wish to speak ill of the nurses, they are only doing their job. In any case, I'm no better at it, to say the least. A simple sock striptease takes me the entire morning. A feat. I should measure the time spent keeping myself clean during my miserable existence. Maintaining my 'personal hygiene' to an acceptable standard for other people. Keeping the mire that threatens to engulf me at bay. For instance, it has become almost impossible for me to wash my back – I am not supple enough and it is most annoying. Or my feet. My fingers seem to be retracting. My hands resemble the webbed feet of a swan. All that remains is for me to bend my neck and pray that I don't feel anything.

The only solution to hand is to soak myself. And wait for the water – the holy water – to do its job. Wait for the mud to dissolve, for the soap to lather. For me to soak until all the shit slides off. Even after my bath, it's better not to get too close. Better not to feel the soft flesh, the hollow bones, the hideous withered skin.

The only attraction of my old carcass is the seam that decorates my chest. A long thick scar that stretches along in the middle of all the folds and cracks. The miracle of the Epiphany.

Of that feast of the Epiphany in 1938 I only remember a few details. It happened a mere stone's throw from here. Outside the entrance to the Denfert metro stop. On the square with the huge statue of a grey muscular lion, a noble beast among the nobility of the Petit-Montrouge district. Le Lion de Belfort is his stage name, and he is staring off in the direction of the New World and Lady Liberty. He is lying down, with his tail suspended in the air. He shows off his splendour pretentiously, towering over the poor mites who walk across the square. He is also called Bartholdi's Lion, after the sculptor who fashioned him, a lion whose powerful paws prop up his powerful breast. His flank is exposed to the elements. His mane resembles a cabaret dancer's hair in her dressing room after the show.

So on that particular feast of the Epiphany, I decided to walk along the Avenue d'Orléans. I stamped on the dead leaves, one by one, as I walked, being careful not to slip because the air was damp. There's nothing more treacherous than damp leaves, as my experience in Ireland, where it rains continuously, proved. In Ireland, my island, where rain is our purgatory.

I walked carefully, covering the dead leaves with my steps, and I thought I was on Baggot Street. The only thing missing was the drunken voices. The singers' voices, which set the guts of the passers-by tingling as the drink burnt their own.

> She died of a fever
> And no one could save her
> And that was the end of sweet Molly Malone.
> Now her ghost wheels her barrow
> Through streets broad and narrow
> Crying 'cockles and mussels alive a-live-O!'

I was taking a little walk – it's an old habit of mine. Walking at twilight. Waiting for dark to fall before drinking. Alan and Belinda expecting me for dinner. For an Irish-style dinner, where we'd drink and tell stories. Alan, as usual, would recite some of Yeats's verses – he recited Yeats, rolling his 'r's:

> A sudden blow: the great wings beating still
> Above the staggering girl, her thighs caressed
> By the dark webs, her nape caught in his bill,
> He holds her helpless breast upon his breast.

He called out my name so I would recite the rest of the poem. The rest of 'Leda and the Swan'. The practice is called 'the noble call', a Dublin form of torture. One name from the assembled party of drinkers is called and the person has to carry on the recital. No refusal is brooked. When I'm called on, I become profoundly embarrassed, to the extent that I can't complete the task that falls to me as a Dubliner. My problem is made greater by the multiple torture sessions – the Irish who love poetry and song are particularly fond of the practice. They never fail to seize the opportunity for a session, and on each occasion my difficulty returns and grows greater. The only remedy that I have found for it is drink. I drink before reciting, when, like the condemned man moving towards the scaffold, the torture is unavoidable. I drink to forget my misfortune at finding myself in the middle of all these laughing men. I drink to forget who I am. It's an Irish solution, if truth be told.

On that particular Epiphany night, it was already late and the waiters were holding our jackets so we could slip them on. The end of the evening was near. We had to go home and that was the hardest thing. Head home in the January cold. Walk past the church of Saint-Pierre-de-Montrouge. Head up the Avenue d'Orléans as far as Impasse Villa Coeur-de-Vey where the Duncans lived.

I had scarcely gone out the door when a man called out to me, he sprang out of nowhere like a jack-in-the-box. He looked like a pimp and he smelled of brothels. A small blond fellow, close-shaven, thin, his overall half-open, he asked me for money and beckoned me to follow him. I don't like being hailed. I mean, even when someone I know meets me on the street, I don't like being hailed. Or being whistled at. If it happens, I pretend that I haven't heard.

And in this particular instance, that's what I did. Since I didn't pay any attention to him, and kept talking to Alan and Belinda, he lost his temper. His unsteady gait indicated to us that he was jittery and by far the most inebriated of us all. He came closer and repeated his disagreeable demand in the following manner:

Don't be tight, give me a few notes. I'll do you a favour and give you a girl for free.

He was getting on my nerves. I asked him, first calmly and then firmly, to get lost. He did nothing of the sort. Continued to wave his arms around and to yammer on. I took a step forward in the direction of the Duncans, whom I had encouraged to keep on walking. The knife, which was stuck in his fist, pulled me up short. The blade made my blood spurt like a geyser. I tried to shout out and then collapsed on the pavement.

Nothing else. Blackness. In the moments that followed, everything went on without me. I was carted off like a corpse drowned in its own juices.

POLICE REPORT

11 January 1938

Following a knife attack that took place on the night of 6–7 January at the intersection between Avenue d'Orléans and Rue Rémy Dumoncel, this morning at around 11 am we arrested the suspect, a certain Robert-Jules Prudent.

Photographs allowed Alan and Belinda Duncan, who had witnessed the attack, and the victim, a 32-year-old Irish citizen, Samuel Barclay Beckett (a writer residing for the last six weeks in the fourteenth district of Paris, at the Liberia Hotel, 9 Rue de la Grande Chaumière), to identify the attacker. The suspect was apprehended in a hotel at 155 Avenue du Maine, where he identified as Germain Prudent. The 25-year-old mechanic is already known to the police as a pimp. Following the attack, he rented a room in the hotel and barricaded himself inside – acquaintances came to bring him food every day.

This morning, after his arrest, he was taken to the Commissariat at Le Petit-Montrouge where he confessed to the crime.

Inspectors Manonvillers, Berthomet,
Grimaldi and Vaizolles

When at last I opened my eyes, I was in an open ward. The court of miracles. There were people all over the place – patients, beds, patients piled onto the beds. Lying on their sides and on their backs and even lying down in the middle of the room. The battered, the dying, the shrivelled. The wails came from all corners of the room. There were bandaged heads where only the eyes, the noses and the waiting mouths were visible. I was in pain. I tried to straighten up under the rough sheets. It was impossible. The patients bleated around me. I wanted to take off. To get away from the suffering plebs whose screams only increased my own feeling of confusion. I could remember nothing. Nothing at all.

I hoped that some bell would help me escape from the nightmare. I searched for a clue that would allow me to know that I was definitely still alive. I was in pain. That was a clue, I was still alive.

At the other end of the big room, a black cape and hat started to dance around the white uniforms. An insect-like silhouette flew in my direction.

'So … You're awake?'

His hands pushed back the little round spectacles that covered his eyes. I was incapable of gathering my thoughts together and so continued to say nothing. My pain was mixed up with my anger at being there, caught up in the misfortune of others who, in turn, saw mine. Joyce was sitting on the bed, his face was all smiles, his eyes beaming as widely as his moustache was narrow; he looked as if he were having a whole lot of fun.

When, that same afternoon, Dr Fontaine came into the room full of moaners, she was in deep conversation with the penman. He had swapped his cape for a sheepskin coat, which, unbuttoned over a waistcoat, also revealed a white shirt and a narrow yellow-and-black striped tie. On his right-hand side he was holding a little lamp. I gazed at them from my bed as if I were watching a show. Joyce had taken off his hat and was holding it in his left hand; his shock of hair was slicked back, forming a little grey hill that dominated his craggy face. I could see that he liked her. It must be said that she had been looking after his ailing eyes for a long time. A writer's eyes are his greatest treasure. Alas, in Joyce's case there was nothing to be done. One day, at her wits' end, she even suggested that he try leeches. And so when I came to visit poor Shem (ungrateful wretch that I was, this was the nickname I liked to give the penman behind his back), the creatures were hopping around his bedroom. The leeches were leaping, Shem was shouting and his son Giorgio was down on his knees trying to pick them up. It was completely mad. The woman is mad. So I was not at all reassured to see her making her way towards me. However, I was aware that I could do nothing other than accept my fate and so I did my best to appear impassive.

'Mr Joyce, I've found a bed for your friend,' she said. 'However, the cost will have to be borne by you.'

Joyce nodded to me. In silence. He showed me the lamp and a manuscript that he took out from under his jacket. As I was being transported to the solitude I had so longed for, I was thinking of only one thing: getting back to work.

ADMISSIONS OFFICE, HÔPITAL BROUSSAIS

Paris, 21 January 1938

Mr Samuel Barclay Beckett
Age: 32
Height: 1.82
Weight: 72 kg
Irish national

The patient was transported to hospital by ambulance in the night of 7 January 1938 at around 4 am, following stabbing and the wound in the pleura having engendered a loss of consciousness.

He came to of his own accord the following day. As he was in no fit state to be transported, the X-ray of the lungs was only performed on 17 January. It confirmed the diagnosis of pleural bleeding, which should be reabsorbed of its own accord. The wound is healing. The lungs are intact.

The patient will be discharged tomorrow, 22 January, with a prescription for rest and antineuralgics. Regular consultations have been scheduled with Dr Fauver or myself at Broussais hospital, and follow-up X-rays and cupping glasses have also been prescribed.

Dr Thérèse Fontaine
Consultant, Paris hospitals

Le Tiers-Temps, Residence for Senior Citizens, Paris

4 August 1989

I followed the rules to the letter. A yellow-and-blue card pinned up in the bathroom gives all the details.

RESIDENTS MUST RESPECT
THE RULES OF ELEMENTARY HYGIENE
AND BODILY CLEANLINESS
COMPATIBLE WITH INSTITUTIONAL LIVING.
MANAGEMENT RESERVE THE RIGHT
TO TAKE ACTION WITH RESIDENTS IF NECESSARY.

Up until now everything had been going swimmingly. The brackish colour of my bathwater bore witness to my good will and my incontrovertible use of soap. Little white scaly bits floated on the surface of the cooling water. Getting out of the bath was another matter entirely. Everything had to be strategically calculated in advance. I had to measure the angles. My main objective was to reach the seat at the other end of the bath. On this point, the instructions are very clear: Exiting the bath means moving *to a seated position on the plastic seat provided for this purpose.*

With the help of an ingenious system thought up by the manufacturers, the aforementioned seat was suspended over the bath itself. An amazing invention on the part of the engineers in the service of the crumblies. And so I grabbed hold of the handle. There were two handles: one fixed on the wall, the other on the edge of the bath; both were mentioned in the instructions described earlier. I lifted myself up and landed with a thump on the seat. Not a spectacular success. Although I did make it safely onto the seat, I must say that my posterior bore the brunt of the thump. I hadn't quite mastered my landing speed or rather my splash landing. I have to admit at the same time that my backside – and its very sharp bones – offered no cushioning. What's more, I feel obliged to explain that far from being a soft comfy chair it was rather hard. I mention it because I'm no longer used to anything hard these days. In any case, moving on.

Once I was sitting on the seat – the suspended seat – I didn't feel too bad. I liked being perched there with my legs still soaking in the soapy water, which was just warm enough for me to feel comfortable. I remained seated there for a while. My calves were fully immersed, the skin on my toes withering. My feet on the rocks at the Forty Foot. I could see my father diving from the men-only bathing area. My brother and I followed him. The thrill of the fall evaporated in water that was as cold as death. We swam like scrawny cuckoos. Our eyes stared at the bay. Buoyed up by the Irish Sea. The cold sea.

Sandycove, Glenageary, Dunleary. I picked up pebbles. I put them in my pockets. I did it so often that there would be holes in my pockets and my mother would scold me. My mother was cold. I kept doing it, though. I couldn't help myself. I stuffed my torn pockets with smooth little pebbles. They would of course fall down my trousers, along my legs. I would pick them up all over again. Dozens of pebbles, tearing holes in my pockets. I thought they would fill the holes. The pebbles would rain down on the grass. Piles of pebbles would make a small sepulchre. A miniature tomb. Ireland's tomb that I left at my feet. At the foot of the tower.

Apparently, the tower is called after Joyce nowadays. Joyce's tower.

Introibo ad altare Dei

That was the start of it for him. Me, I got off to a bad start – my starts left much to be desired. It's important to get off to a good start. I got off to a bad start in Ireland. In actual fact, I left much to be desired and had to leave. Had to come back. Several times. I left so often that I never came back.

I had to come up with an exit strategy. Even the best baths come to an end. I moved my legs, pointed them in another direction and managed to reach the steps for the elderly that had been placed in front of the bath to help me. I was nothing like Degas's dancers going up the stairs, their lithe legs barely touching the stage with their pointe shoes. Nothing like them. Nothing at all.

*

This morning an unidentified individual entered my room. An acolyte of the type that usually teaches me to stand upright on my own two feet. Apparently, it had all been arranged. Well. He had barely set foot in my den when he started laying down the law:

'Mr Beckett, we're going to test your balance.' He added, in order to reassure me: 'Don't worry, it's easy, all you have to do is follow my instructions.'

First hurdle. Since childhood, when anyone employs a certain tone of voice to ask me to do something, I think that I am instantly obeying orders, whereas in actual fact quite the opposite happens. It may even happen that, entirely accidently, I start to do the opposite without even being aware of what's going on. Now, I know that means people think I am pulling their leg. Most of the time, it couldn't be farther from the truth. I try to do my best. But my limbs won't obey me. They undermine my good faith. They plunge me into contradictory currents and leave me adrift in an ocean of contradictions. As a child, I often paid the price for such behaviour. My ears are still burning because of it. I often paid the price for it. It's not my fault. I was a kind of nuisance – a pain in the neck, as I was called at home. I was an awkwardly placed shard. Very awkward. I am the first to admit to it, without being able to do anything about it. So, because I was aware of this congenital defect, I didn't approach the famous test with the same boundless enthusiasm as my interlocutor – an enthusiasm that I linked on his part to his absolute ignorance of the dangers life holds in store for us, that allow little room for us to be overly enthusiastic. In any case.

The enthusiast was very well built, hairy as a yeti, with chest hair overflowing from his press-buttoned tunic. A booming voice emerged from his larynx, using nuances of language which I was not sure I quite understood. He made a point of taking out a big notebook from which hung a transparent retractable red ballpoint pen, before pronouncing the following enigmatic sentence:

'Off you go, Mr Beckett, this a test of your balance based on the Berg Balance Scale.' He felt it necessary to complete the sentence with the following turn of phrase: 'Let's get the show on the road, Joe.'

Since he had given me no precise instructions as to the movements he wanted me to perform, and had failed to identify the Joe in question, I decided not to take issue with the overfamiliar form of address that the yeti had employed (was he himself the Joe in question? That was what I had begun to believe), thinking that there was, all things considered, a form of coherence between the body and mind of the creature.

We had scarcely got started with the exercises when the beast went at it again, suggesting a whole range of physical jerks, which I undertook with the good faith of a holy communicant.

'Mr Beckett, please stand up without using your hands.'

I gave it a go and just about caught myself in time. Tried again. Failed again. No better.

'Wait a second, I'm ticking the box for *Can stand up unaided, aided by his hands*. Off we go again. Get the show on the road.'

God save us from another rhyme.

'Now, try to stay upright for two minutes without leaning on anything. Take your hands away … There you are. Not bad at all, Mr Beckett! We can do the same thing now with your eyes closed.'

Did the beast think I was some sort of nymphet who had just signed up for his gym class? I dropped my arms in dismay – and of course I should have done nothing of the sort. Nothing of the sort. My arms were to enter into the danse macabre my torturer had ordered for me.

'Lift your arms at a ninety-degree angle. Spread out your fingers as far forward as possible. Mind your leaning points, Mr Beckett, we don't want you to fall.'

I am one of those who fall, I thought. Those who collapse, roll under the furniture, slide down the hills. I favour the fall. There we go, an alliteration. I have always favoured the fall. In Foxrock, I used to fall from the tops of the trees, expecting that the outstretched branches of the big pine tree – my final safety net – would catch me in extremis. Before the fall, I could hear the wind high up there and the pine needles trembling. I rocked back and forth with them, faster and faster, like a featherless bird, until I was carried away on my own momentum. I fell and fell farther. I was always revived. Knocked myself out and started again. A thousand ends, from which I emerged unscathed. Unfit for dying. Bad fall. Not yet the end.

*

Yesterday, when it was time for my long-awaited walk, and as I was about to slip on my jacket, I was scolded – return to childhood – by a certain 'Jacqueline' (or perhaps she was called Catherine, I tend to get the two names mixed up). Be that as it may, the lady started her accusations, claiming that I had filled my trouser pockets with the toast from breakfast. Not only was I guilty of not feeding myself enough but I was also guilty of scandalously wasting food, she said. The presence of toast in my pockets had led to a whole series of problems of which I seemed to be incapable of measuring the consequences and on which I was now to inform myself in detail.

The rules state that *Residents' personal laundry is washed and ironed within the establishment*, and so my toast-laden trousers had landed, without being searched beforehand (because we are short of time, she said, 'can you imagine how long it would take if we had to turn out everyone's pockets', etc. etc.), in the middle of everyone else's laundry. My trousers had thus trailed crumbs all over the rags of my fellow residents and, it would appear, might have damaged the Tiers-Temps washing machine, which was almost new – because it had been purchased only a few months ago – had the household staff not immediately undertaken a thorough cleaning of the filters. The contravention was unforgivable and never to be repeated.

Having been made aware of the gravity of the offence I had unknowingly committed, I came to the conclusion that I would have to offer my humblest apologies or else it would be impossible for me to escape. Alas, I was not allowed the time to do so. The prosecutor was so happy to have it out with me that she went on to say that in case I felt like arguing with her, all laundry was clearly marked with the residents' names (article 12.2 of house rules, in the subsection devoted to *Laundry and other sundries*), and she was therefore in possession of the offending item, a pair of trousers marked with the initials *SB*.

It was the straw that broke the camel's back. Too many useless words. I decided to throw in the towel. My legs no longer allowed me to take off when danger or disagreeable things were near. Several months earlier, I already had to perfect the following strategy: when somebody was getting on my wick, the only real tactic that old people can deploy is that of playing dead or attempting some passive form of resistance. For my part, being unable to carry out the first tactic, I catch hold of my oxygen mask, lie down on my bed, pretend I am worn out and close my eyes. The effect is immediate. The attacker has to dial things down, especially if they are a member of the staff, and, as this is the most favourable outcome, they usually say nothing more.

And this was in fact what happened. The dragon in her apple-green tunic finished her phrase and left. I put my hand in my pocket and felt the crumbs of the day in my trousers. That was how things were. I share my breakfast with the pigeons or with whatever bird happens to be passing by. Is that so terrible? In Greystones I used to throw crumbs out of the kitchen window. The house was on the way to the cemetery at Bray Head, and I could see the rooks with their pointy beaks pecking to the north. I threw the crumbs and the roundy outlines of the song thrushes were the only ones to dare draw near. In the drawing room, the only music we could hear was the crackling of the wireless. One day it crackled the war into our ears. The ears of my mother, and my own ears. Chamberlain declared war, in English, in our drawing room: *We and France are today, in fulfilment of our obligations, going to the aid of Poland, who is so bravely resisting this wicked and unprovoked attack on her people.*

May stared at the cemetery on Bray Head, as I readied myself to leave. To head off head first, my beak pointing at the continent. Heading straight off, as was my wont, straight for trouble.

*

In general, when I got ready to leave, something always happened – something akin to the invisible hand of fate – which seemed to hold me back. For the longest time, I thought my mother was at fault. The cold dead hand of May pulled the invisible strings, so that a whole host of obstacles impeded my departure. On that very day, my mother was disguised as a civil servant from Newhaven, where I had disembarked with the hope of heading to France. I recognized her under the peaked cap of the customs agent who forbade me to leave, forbade me to join the service of the country whose habits I had adopted, more than anyone else, for good or ill, and whose language I had made my own. 'Whose very language,' I repeated to him. He refused to listen.

'Your papers?' he said.

I did not have the document that allowed me to leave the territory, a document which, one after the other, the other passengers displayed; he would not listen to anything I said. When he saw the mention of the word 'Irish' on my papers, the pencil-pusher felt suddenly inspired. There followed a conversation which included whiskey, the shamrock and the Holy Trinity. I submitted as serenely as possible to the agonies it entailed. It must be said that the taciturn, of whom I am one, in general have an inordinate ability to find themselves face to face with individuals whose peculiar talent is to say as little as possible in as many words as they possess. I was waiting for someone to rescue me, to offer me an escape route, or any way out at all. Although I had my doubts on the issue, I was even prepared to envisage the hypothesis of a miracle; that will tell you how difficult I felt my situation was. The miracle occurred – God knows why. The stamp came down on my documents. No man was ever so happy to enter a country at war.

'Mr Beckett, if you'd like to go out, you need to leave now, afterwards it will be dinner time.'

The door was half-open. No dragon in sight, the coast was clear. Off I go, I thought, and I leaned with difficulty on the table. And then I was away, my hands in my swollen pockets. Swollen with toast.

*

On my way back from my little jaunt (what an exaggeration!), a typewritten note awaited me on the table. It was addressed to all 'residents' – another exaggerated term, it should have read 'old things who wander the corridors while hanging on to the walls, and wearing out the lino with their walking sticks. Or Kings of the walkers. Apostles of the wheelchairs. Phoenixes of the false teeth'? They could have livened it up a bit, used some imagination, for heaven's sake! Terminology. Nevertheless, the high priestess of Le Tiers-Temps – described by all as a charming woman who, apparently, likes Schubert – was writing to the residents (that is to say ourselves) about television sets. Her prose began thus:

Residents may bring their own television and radio sets, however, the volume of the aforementioned sets should under no circumstances disturb other residents.

Thus far, no problem. Although I may be reticent with regard to the be-chignoned dowager who has the room next to mine – my conversations with her usually happen at a very high pitch and she gets worked up very early in the morning – I thank God that I don't also have to put up with the rumblings of her television set. The colony of hearing-aid wearers is frequently followed by 'staff' who encourage them to move to the common room so they can watch their programmes together in a convivial fashion. This suits me down to the ground.

Ah! I notice that a *nota bene* has been added to the end of the page. This is unusual.

For the V Nations Championship currently being broadcast, the establishment will make portable black-and-white television sets available to residents in exchange for a deposit. They will be able to keep the sets in their rooms while the programme is being broadcast and should then return them to reception. Thank you for your co-operation. Kind regards, the management.

Jesus! And here was I, still boasting about being an atheist!

*

[Television set]

'They are going to go all the way! And Serge Blanco touches down between the posts! Extraordinary! The French are back in the match! What a turnaround! A try that came from the back of the field again! With the help of Franck Mesnel at the 22-metre line, and which miraculously ends up in Serge Blanco's hands! And France has scored their third try of the match! What a try from the French team! There were fifteen passes in this phase and Serge Blanco was there to bring it home, what a symbol! He has just scored his eightieth try of the tournament. Which means that he has become the all-time best try scorer for France!

Let's have another look at Franck Mesnel's counterattack, which was helped by the forward. Portolan was central to this phase – as you can see, he is at the halfway line. Blanco's counterattack, then Caminati and on to Lafond who avoids a tackle; he is helped by Blanco and Rodriguez. And look who is here, Portolan is back again, fifty metres further on, and the Irish are not in place. Things are not going well for the Irish. The cat's among the pigeons or, as we say in France, the pig is in the clover.

And the Irish have the ball again. Aherne doesn't control the ball and Berbizier gets it, well done! With Carminati who has the support of Ondarts; Ondarts drives on. And he turns around, the ball goes to Berbizier, Berbizier passes it to Mesnel, and the ball goes all the way to Blanco, Blanco passes to Lagisquet! Will he go all the way? Yes! Another try for *the French team! And the French team takes the lead. What a comeback!*

Jean-Baptiste Lafond's conversion goes over the bar. Two more points! And France leads by twenty-six to twenty-one for Ireland, with only seven minutes left to play. What an extraordinary turnaround when the score was fifteen–nil! At one stage it was even twenty-one–seven. What a comeback! And the match is over! Unbelievable!'

Christ on a bike! I have difficulty believing it myself. Useless men in green. Only good for picking potatoes. The pig is in clover and he caught up with them all right, and ate them out of house and home. There's nothing left to look forward to except a good long famine. It won't be their first. They're all descended from the Great Hunger, escaped from the mildew. How was it they didn't feel the wind as he whistled past?

Good God, I wish I still had legs like them. I wasn't a bad runner in my day when I did have legs. I galloped like a hare, with my skinny elastic shanks. Number twelve or thirteen. Always in the centre. Ready to use my hands and my legs. Wandering off to the side. Known for my wandering. My knees to the sky, my eyes on the grass, ready to dive, keeping my eyes on the fine calves to chase, to catch. Tackling to the ground, flat out on the pitch. Until the prop falls over and his powerless hands open and release the oval ball.

Tick, tack, to the left, to the right. I avoided the tackler and kicked. Headed off into the fog until a shadow stopped my mad run, caught me at the waist and brought me down to eat the short grass. Trapped under the colossus, I prayed for the game to end. For the whistle to be blown. And then I collapsed onto the daisies, swearing that it was my last match. They were all the same as the previous one and, alas, it was never my last.

Le Tiers-Temps, Residence for Senior Citizens, Paris
5 August 1989

Earlier on, the nurse, Nadja (what a name!) with her beautiful fern-coloured eyes, knocked at my door. She was worried about me, about how much I was eating. Or rather, how little.

'Skinny as a rake,' she said to me. 'Nothing new,' I said to her. *Skinny as a rail*, was what my mother used to say. As thin as a railway line, a twig, a piece of spaghetti, a stalk, a slat in a boarding-school bed. *A skeleton!* May would shout when I pulled on my shorts, which displayed my long legs and knobbly knees. A two-dimensioned chap, thin as cigarette paper.

My response didn't fluster Nadja. It took a lot more to make her lose her cool. I don't know how much more, but more in any case. She stared at me through my glasses with her fern-coloured eyes and announced, as if it were an event of considerable importance, that *she had suggested to the doctor that he should review my diet*. And she wanted to *outline the decisions taken* so that I should not be surprised by *the new content of the menus intended for me over the coming days*. What wonderful reading material.

From my point of view, I have never been able to understand people's habits round here, as I consider that the more time you spend eating the less you have for drinking. An Irish perspective on the world, I grant you. Nosh is not my favourite terrestrial nourishment – other food has offered me greater sustenance. That's my view.

Nadja began her speech with some little verbal sleights of hand, assuring me that of course *no one in the residence questioned my capacity to feed myself in an autonomous fashion.* She laid great stress on the word 'capacity', as if it were a kind of accomplishment, for an old lump of a man like myself to peck away at things on my own. She underlined the fact that I ate *without making a mess*, and pointed to my dexterity with a fork. She went on in that vein for a while and as she did so I asked myself: how had it come to this? How had life led me, in such an underhand manner, to become a character plucked from my own delirium, my own nightmares? Shambling Sam, with his head lolling in his soup, toothless Sam. Pozzo's Lucky for whom there is little else in store. I nodded off as the beauty went on with her beautiful speech. When I managed to focus again, the tone of her commentary had changed.

'Over the past few days, Mr Beckett, the staff have noticed that your tremor has been stopping you from cutting your meat, opening your yoghurt or peeling your fruit. And so you leave those items on your tray perhaps because you are afraid of making a mess.'

64

As I failed to respond she continued, unperturbed: 'The doctor has suggested that we adapt your meals and that additional nutriments should also be administered by injection. Here are your menus for tomorrow. Lunch: thickened vegetable soup; grated cheese; scrambled eggs mixed with milk; enriched vanilla cream (plus nutritional oral supplements). Evening meal: cereal soup with protein powder; vegetable and potato purée (milk and butter); stewed fruit with cottage cheese.'

Never had the horizon felt as low. My life is as constricted as my gullet. I looked at Nadja and thought of your man, André Breton, who had seen eyes *open mornings on a world where the beating of hope's great wings is scarcely distinct from the other sounds which are those of terror*. The terror had beautiful fern-coloured eyes, she was buzzing in my ears.

*

After lunch, I had a look at the notes that hang from the end of my bed. A delightful read. Mr Beckett finished his dish, went for his walk and we changed his bedding – stories worthy of *Countess Poo-poo*. The life of a biped written down in a big green notebook, slipped into a plastic file. It's come to this. Victor wild boy of the Aveyron, grown old, scrutinized through a spyglass of Doctor Itard.

Some of the passages are worth their weight in tin: the aerosol 'flow rate' and that of the mushroom soup. Memorable. I'm not far from the dustbin. Actually, I'm completely inside the dustbin.

The presentation page is quite perfunctory. Bad start. Lack of style. Things could have been spelled out at greater length. It could have been noted that the aged male is of Irish extraction, that he has thick black-and-white hair. What else? The animal is solitary, not very aggressive. Above all, he does not wish to be disturbed.

However, on the whole there is nothing to be added. The beast is examined from all angles: speed of displacement, adaptation to his habitat. There is an incomparable attention to detail. An assessment of what remains. No glory in the findings: lung function mediocre, genuflectory capacities far lower than expected from one raised as a believer – even a Protestant believer; weak as water. The same questions constantly elicit the same responses, recorded in minute detail – the official archive of advanced age.

Nothing about the old man's physique. There are things to be said, no doubt about that: endless wrinkles, a neck like a turkeycock, not one of his teeth his own. A Goya portrait, skin on bones, a dark background of greys and greens. The old fellow is sitting in front of his bowl of soup. His cachectic hand lifts the spoon with difficulty, his mouth closed in a rictus. He repeats the movements of the meal: the spoon, the soup. His jaundiced eyes contemplate the shadow of death that beckons. The soup is served, he doesn't swallow it. He waits to feel a little better.

Those pink slips, I know what they mean. They are the 'travel chits'. How I go, where I go. Who accompanies me where. Apart from a couple of walks around the block, I need to be pushed and pulled. In fact, as the form states, I arrived in the holy home by ambulance. Always in an ambulance. It's unavoidable. No matter what happens, I always end up in an ambulance. In the past I rode up front, now I'm in the back.

Long ago, I crossed Paris as if it were an open grave while the injured were rolled up in their blankets. It was wartime, and the crippled, maimed and mutilated needed to be driven round. I pushed forward until there was pushback. Until the debacle. Until the jackboots clicked and clacked across the city. Until they kept everything underfoot. Until darkness fell. As members of the Resistance, we moved to pull the wool over the enemy's eyes – we were PI agents in the service of His Glorious Majesty. Pushing messages into matchboxes. Pushing British strategy.

One day we were almost pushed into oblivion. We had to run. The traitor's name was Robert. Robert Alesch, traitor–priest. Great sinner. He was pushing for pennies and preaching for pounds. My friends fell. I left. And went into hiding.

Le Tiers-Temps, Residence for Senior Citizens, Paris
6 August 1989

Lucia's letters fell off the shelves. They were stuck between Wilde and Joyce, between Kafka and Yeats. Yellowed scrawls, crumpled pages, dating from the era when Lucia wrote from behind unbreachable doors. Between two injections. Between two therapy sessions. Between two exiles. Nyon, Küsnacht, Ivry, Pornichet, Burghölzi ... From one lunatic asylum to the next, Lucia circled purgatory. The eternal prisoner.

Every week, I would travel to the Orléans-Ceinture railway station, with its pink bricks and white merlons. I took the 1.44 pm train, arrived in Ivry an hour later. Lucia was slipping deeper and deeper into herself. The cloister would be her tomb. Little by little, the tongues became connected. The words left her. Everyone left her. Yet voices continued to speak to her, she told me. I also spoke to her. She didn't answer. What could she hear among the stifled shouts and the silent straitjackets? I don't know. They all left her. She could feel them leaving her. She could feel herself leaving too. Lucia was lost in the desert. They were only two souls who could still breach the doors – her father and myself. Her Babbo Joyce and Sam. On 13 January 1941 her father died – no more Babbo, no more Joyce. It was wartime. He died in the middle of the dead. One more. Lucia read in the newspaper that he had left us. That he had left her. She withdrew a little more. Withdrew into silence.

Lucia's letters are out again, they have fallen from the shelf. They lie between the book covers. Between Joyce and Wilde.

> The wild bee reels from bough to bough
> With his furry coat and his gauzy wing.
> Now in a lily-cup, and now
> Setting a jacinth bell a-swing,
> In his wandering;

They are all gone. Suzanne. Wilde, Joyce, Lucia. They are all gone. I have to remind myself, all the time.

ACT TWO

Le Tiers-Temps, Residence for Senior Citizens, Paris

9 August 1989

The loony next door is wailing again. She sings every morning during her ablutions – it's a regular occurrence. As if turning on the tap also turned on the sound in her throat; she pulls the chain and out it flows. Two turns to the right and she's off – childhood airs, autumnal airs, shampooing the hair. As the temperature gets hotter, the old one gets more carried away – the hotter it gets the higher she goes, and her voice is index-linked to the humidity in the room. In the upper registers, the old cow varies the range and the repertoire, alternating between happy and sad songs. Her voice overflows, floods, sinks like boots into the mud; it travels through the partition, revives bitter memories. Until the stopper is pulled and the merwidow's chorus, memorializing her fate amongst her fellow merwidows, dies away. And silence roars once again. The noisy silence of old age in its final resting place.

After the war, May was watchful behind her window. She didn't sing – she never sang or very rarely, perhaps in church, opening her mouth thus, closing it immediately again. From her post behind the window, she didn't sing; she did nothing, she trembled at the sight of the mountains. Her eyes were as big as saucers, as big as the saucers that chinked in her hands, against which, in spite of herself, she made the teaspoons clink. My mother's blue eyes devoured the outdoors. She nourished them through the Foxrock window. She nourished them with passing life. With back-and-forths. People promenaded past the brand-new shack. The shack built for her old age. Facing east, into her memories. Always on the road. *The prison of memory*, she used to say. Like the wind that blows the dead branches, ready to fall, the light ones that rest on the living in the hope of holding them back, my mother's trembling hands were placed on the pane of glass in the hope that the pane might keep them in place. To no avail. The iron fist was now so shaky that the crepuscular castle had in turn become unsteady. The wind of the war that had not taken place at home had nonetheless blown its incurable sadness onto the backs of the survivors. My mother was ageless. She was as old as her frocks, as old as the world. She was like a dried-out apple. She acted as a sentry, and trembled one last time before petrifying in front of the window. Her smile was absent, her hearing faulty; she was waiting for the end.

There were good sides to this. More than before. May had become a snake without the venom, a billy goat without horns, a fallen heroine. She was unrecognizable.

One day, I went into my mother's bedroom. It was an ordinary room, the furniture long ago infested with woodworm.

How might it be described? Perhaps I should start at the back of the room with the dressing table that was covered with fake white marble on which a brass bowl stood and into which a vase was placed. Old rites. Washing and pissing, one fitting into the other. And in the air, the tainted smell of a body disintegrating, falling apart, losing itself in its own farts, under the amused gaze of the wallpaper flowers. A single bed was flush with that wall, the size reflected the chastity that was henceforth hers. A widow's solitude, married to death. Her brass bed, greyish-green from mutual contamination, the oxidation of the mattress by its ancient owner. Nothing else to be said about it, other than to note the lair's darkness. My mother's lair, my mother's breast. The darkness of May who fed my own darkness, who had sown the *fleurs malad-ives*, the sickly flowers. Nursed until I had received the last drop of bile, I lay for a long time on her bed of sadness. For a long time, I felt that I had no choice but to do battle with the demons who devoured my spleen. *Silence*, the melan-choly voices murmured in my ear. But on that particular Thursday – I believe is was a Thursday – in my mother's room, the vision was entirely different. For the first time, my eyes had grown accustomed to the darkness, May's darkness and my own – May's darkness which had become mine – opening onto buried worlds. My vision had become clear. A primeval scene, primitive as if a window had opened onto an empty, desiccated landscape, a country road at nightfall, which promised only a hazy perilous adventure which I had shied away from until now. As an undertaker's assistant, all that was left for me to do was dig until it filtered in. Scrape away until I reached the bottom. Enter the obscurity, follow the tunnel. Discover the bodies trapped there and shake off the dust of dreams. Overflowing with the fire of the beyond, I was close to the precipice, right on the edge. Although I was overcome by vertigo, the pit offered the best of remedies. The best for me. Like the shadows in the morning, which capture both the obscurity of the night and the light of the coming day, I was alone, like a horseman on my mount, drunk with joy and sadness. Ready to head off again. To wash up on the arid, deserted lands of the survivors. To bury myself in the sand, head first, right up to the rump, digging the soil with my mouth. With a tongue that was not mine.

Le Tiers-Temps, Residence for Senior Citizens, Paris

11 August 1989

Woken up this morning by a friendly toothache. *Good morning, Cavity. You old rotter.* Third molar from the back on the right-hand side. Sam is fed up to his eye teeth. As toothless as a hen. More French than ever.

That old ache – it never leaves me. A pain that comes back to haunt me. A haunting memory. It was after the war. It was no panacea. Hunger caused toothache. Lack of mastication. Teeth laid off temporarily, unfulfilled. They started to work again slowly around the family table, *crunch, scrunch.* In Ireland, they were called into action again. Meat pies and beer; boxty and Irish stew.

Around the table they were kept busy. I mean – there were lots of people. I met my old friends again: MacGreevy, Jack and Cottie, my pals hadn't changed. I was a little less Sam: white hair, thinner, toothaches. In any case, I was no more than myself. Whereas Jack was still Yeats's brother; he was in his workshop. He was painting. A large canvas that was green and electric blue. A Celtic legend. On the canvas, Jack painted Diarmuid, lord of hell, electric lord, Diarmuid running off with Gráinne, the beloved of Finn. In the painting, Finn has caught up with Diarmuid and Gráinne. Diarmuid is going to die. Just beforehand, as he lies on the ground, he is waiting for Finn to give him the last handful of water. That's what Jack wanted to paint. Hope suspended. Thirst. The end. Jack's Diarmuid has a blue face. He is looking at the water and his hope is running through Finn's hands. The end is nigh and it is blue.

On the boat, the blue of the end pursued me. The blue in Jack's painting. When I reached Saint-Lô – the capital of the ruins – death was still there, like a throbbing pain. Blasted tooth. I was driving through the ruins and the mud. Ambulances and Red Cross vans. We wore the cross for those who had nothing left to wear. The collapsed, the sagging, the half-naked injured tangled up in the rubble. The dreadful mud swallowed them up. I drove like the clappers towards Dieppe or Cherbourg – the nurses were afraid I'd crash. But I didn't. I didn't in Saint-Lô, either. I was almost the only driver on the roads. I drove so fast that they would hang onto the handles – the grab-handles – for dear life. Hung onto them and closed their eyes tight until we arrived. As for me, I drove fast so that I wouldn't have to see the surroundings, the ruined landscape, through the dirty windscreen. The spectacle of stones, cinders and ruins. Nothing worse than cinders – ashes to ashes, the infernal cycle. The dross of a disappeared civilization, floating on the surface of a darkish pool. Personal effects, the only touches of colour: blue work clothes, brown bootees, disembowelled straw chairs. The stones themselves were split. Saint-Lô destroyed was the kingdom of the shattered. Ninety-five per cent of it was flattened.

I felt my eyes cracking behind their pebble-thick lenses. They were opening for the first time on a chaos I know only within myself. The distress lurking there, engrained there, a far greater misery than my own. A hodgepodge of intertwined misery, melted on the ground in Saint-Lô. The ruins of the war – the debris of D-Day, of the battle that happened in July. Saint-Lô had received a more than generous share of bombs. They had rained down on it, and it bore the misery of the world as a result. First the train station, then the electricity station. Saint-Lô lit up like a fireworks display. A theatre of torpedoes and reconquest.

When we landed – a terrifying memory – the feathered creatures of misfortune were flying above the crippled victims that were vomited onto the streets of Saint-Lô in their hundreds. The half-dead, the almost victims, the almost-nothing-no-more who were trying to cover themselves and who were no longer protected by anything. Not even by the decapitated church. Nor by the calcinated trees, nor by the few buildings that remained standing, waiting for a breath of wind to blow them down. Nothing remained. Just the endless drizzle of tears that rained down from the sky on the town. Rained down on Saint-Lô.

The rest of us – nurses, ambulance drivers, doctors without remedies – Irish Samaritans, arrived one day in August 1945 to build a hospital there. We bandaged the wounds and poured libations of oil and wine. Irish Samaritans always pour wine. For themselves and for others. That's how it is. The wine flowed in the evening when the wooden huts that served as a hospital were at rest. When the patients slept. One of the huts was lined with aluminium – it was Dr McKee's makeshift operating theatre. A theatre where miracles were performed. In the corridors, Dr Arthur Darley (otherwise known as A.D.) took out his violin. A.D. was born in a violin – his father's violin had travelled round the world a hundred times by the force of his fingers alone. A.D. heated up the huts with violin music and calvados. We drank the calvados that the hordes of patients gave us each day as an offering in exchange for every miracle performed. A.D. the humble saviour, doctor of the poor by day, made up for it each night by getting drunk. As soon as the moon appeared, A.D.'s old demons took possession of his body. Took possession of the bodies of the harlots, transformed misery into ecstasy. A.D. exulted until dawn. Until dawn, A.D. was someone else. In the morning, he became *Dr Darley* once more. Contrite, he took up *Lives of the Saints* and his patients once more. A.D. was not the only one to go to the brothel, we would all go there. In Saint-Lô, it was the brothel that helped us survive. The forbidden fruit that we could bite.

It would be difficult to bite anything today. An old wreck. My dentition is past its sell-by date – a capital of ruins. A coherent ensemble. The cavity has been almost completely destroyed – ninety-five per cent. Throbbing pain. Always in pain.

'Mr Beckett, for your toothache I've put a 1000 mg tablet of paracetamol on your tray. The dentist will see you tomorrow morning at eight o'clock. You'll see, he is very kind.'

Let's hope he doesn't bite.

At dawn, the hour the dentist bleaches, curled up in my armchair, I know what awaits me. The torture of the drill bit that spins very fast and the gentle pissing of the jet of water that accompanies it. Concentrating hard, I recite verses in my head that have been resonating there for a long time. Ronsard – I've always called him 'Ronnesaw', the difficulty for an anglophone to distinguish between 'on' and 'r' should not be underestimated. This is one of the holy grails of exile. Ronnesaw rings in my head, to an air of whistling hydraulics. The lines refer to Hélène – it's often about Hélène:

> *Quand vous serez bien vielle, au soir à la chandelle,*
> *Assise auprès du feu, dévidant et filant,*
> *Direz chantant mes vers, en vous émerveillant :*
> *Ronsard me célébrait du temps que j'étais belle.*

> When you are very old, sitting in the evening by
>   candlelight,
> Beside the fire, winding and spinning,
> You will say, full of wonder, as you sing my verses:
> Ronsard celebrated me when I was beautiful.

Devilish 'Ronnesaw'. Cranky. Nasty. Could have been English. I could never invent nasty characters. Always mad. Sometimes old. But not nasty, or no nastier than the next fellow. I would have liked to do them though. I would have liked the grand gougers to visit me on the page. Have them fill my works with venom and gall. They never showed.

When I wrote, when I wrote to my heart's content, I mean, it was after the war. I wrote at home, in Paris or in Ussy. This was my method: I would sit down in the evening at my table and imagine a huge ear behind me – a huge ear, accompanied by a huge mouth, a very beautiful mouth – that listened to me. It listened to the words come into my head as I wrote, and it gave me its opinion. I trusted it, up to a point, I listened to it. It would say, *That's not bad*, so I would continue with my writing, I would write: '*C'était sur une route d'une nudité frappante*,' it liked it and so I continued. Sometimes, I didn't know whether it was listening to me or whether I was listening to it and writing what it said. I was mixed up. I was mixed up even more because, for reasons that have remained mysterious, it spoke with a slight Dublin accent. Not a south County Dublin accent – not a posh accent that came from the back of the throat and ended up in the nose, no, I could never have tolerated that. And it wasn't the northside accent either, the one that puts fuck in the middle of every second word and swears even when its mouth is closed. It was a little high-pitched accent that rose and fell. An old lady's accent. A nineteenth-century accent. It was perfect for prose, that little accent. It spoke for me, for the amnesiacs, the crippled on crutches, the bedridden. For the hordes of lawmen, for the indispensable civil servants, for the big fat women, for social workers. The accent was everything and its opposite. It was all characters at once. Sometime it could eat people up and spit them out. That didn't bother me. Somebody needed to organize my story. It could eat them up. Unlike me.

'You can rinse out your mouth now, Mr Beckett. You can spit into the basin to your right.'

If that makes him happy. I have nothing against it. I hawk and spit with gusto. The pleasures of an old smoker. A gob of spit from my gob. My tongue falls into the hole where the molar was. Down the back on the right-hand side. A new chasm.

They weren't lying when they said that the dentist was very kind, and very handsome too – I noticed it, even though usually all those things are beyond me, especially where dentists are concerned. *A handsome man*, Suzanne would have said to annoy me. And it did annoy me a little when she said *A handsome man* or *What a handsome man*. However, I knew her well enough to know that her intention was to annoy me. It should have slid off me like water off a duck's back, like the ducks that float on the pond in Stephen's Green on a Sunday in October while the leaves fall gently all around them. No, I have to say that it didn't run off me. In actual fact, quite the opposite. It stuck to me. Stuck on tight, kept me stuck in a right mood. In actual fact, it was because I knew that she said *What a handsome man* with the intention of annoying me to high heaven that I actually got myself into such a state. High heaven and beyond. I was a bit of a ladies' man myself. She was tormented by it. That was how things were. It tormented her, so she would say *What a handsome man* about the dentist or anyone else, hoping to get revenge. Revenge was a dish she seasoned and served as payback for my escapades. *Escapades*, what a great word. As if she could have expected anything else from a man who had no beliefs. Who ended up on earth by accident and who remained there out of negligence. Who pretended to forget the solitude to which he was condemned since he had failed his entrée into this world. A man who drifted along, side by side, with other men, not quite of this world, not quite beyond it. A man who was more solitary than a rat, but who wished to be beyond all those concerns.

The *handsome man* drew nearer to the white leather chair that generously accommodated my person, his mask pulled down over his chin. He took off on a long rant – about my mouth and its contents – of which I caught only the conclusion:

'I took the opportunity, while you were under anaesthetic, to take out the filling – it was very old – and pull out the tooth. I'll put in an implant in a few days' time, when your gum has healed.'

The dentist is such a handsome man. And so skilful. The sea of pain has receded. The dental revolt has been quashed. For a while. At last I will be able to sleep. Sleep, nothing more.

Le Tiers-Temps, Residence for Senior Citizens, Paris

12 August 1989

[Garden side]

Who will we put in Normandy? Madame Mélinge, you're going to Normandy? One, two, three, four … What about you? Do you want to go to Brittany? Or to the north? Madame Colard, you go there. Madame Lecoq, you can settle over there with the Bretons. The teams are ready. Each of us is going to select two boules. Madame Colard, you start … Well done! Ten points. Let's have another try, an extra one. Wonderful! And the same goes for the shuffleboard. Everyone can have two throws. Go on, Madame Joffrin, a warm-up throw? Oh, ONE, it's not much but it counts all the same because it's on the right colour. Five, six, seven, eight, well done you Bretons! Perhaps some of you would prefer to go mini-bowling and there's also a pool table at the bottom of the garden …

In the end, the women, those silly geese, woke me up. Not surprising, it's Saturday, market day. Games for silly geese right under my windows. What time is it? Ten o'clock. I slept well. I dreamed. I dreamed of home. Of my house, of cocks and orchards. Of the hills painted by Hayden, my dearest comrade, my lost comrade. The solicitor is coming on Monday, that must be it. I dreamed of my house in Ussy-sur-Marne. Ussy, my elsewhere. I walked in the hills, my pockets full of sweets. I emptied them into the hands of the children in the Molien orchards. I emptied them until there were none left. I walked across the soil as quick as I could, like a madman. I walked along the dung-encrusted paths, the mud forming crusts on the bottom of my trouser legs. I walked and was as dirty as a muck savage, wrapped up in my big Aran sweater, happy to bury myself at Ussy – right up to the neck. I dreamed of my house. The white house. On the apple and pear trails, towards Avernes or Beauval, a little house where it was good to cloister. Before this one, there were others – there were always others.

In August I would leave grotty Paris, sweaty Paris, for Ussy. I would go and meet Hayden. My white house didn't exist yet. I used to camp out at the Café de la Marne, Rue de Changis, opposite the church, in a little niche. Hayden painted the café. Dark interior. Pistachio-green walls. The wooden counter was adorned with a bright-blue rug. On the rug was a tray covered with grey felt and three dice. Dice for games of Buck Dice. I never played it – I only played chess with Hayden – but I remember it. I used to look at the lads throwing dice. Burly lads from the village. Jacques and his brother Dédé the Dice. They used to like playing, I think. I remember the dice sitting on the counter, next to the bottles. The lads had only to throw and pray, for a mulligan or a big buck.

Hayden used to like the felt mat and the dice. He liked them; he painted them. He also painted the yellow triangular ashtray (aniseed yellow, if memory serves me), the heavy blue glasses and the bottles on the counter. He painted them and added a pipe made of light-coloured wood – that touched his nose when he put it in his mouth and his eyes shone like lava in the middle of a smoking volcano. Hayden's light, brilliant clarity, a cream-coloured sun rising over a symphony of green hills, the middle-sized mountains of the Marne. Hayden was day and I was night.

I always went back to Ussy. I went back there when the sun was high and my nerves were taut. Not to the café any more. But to a house. The Barbiers' house, which I rented for a few kopecks. Hayden was never far off, a couple of pedal-strokes away. Hayden in the Marne, where he had taken refuge with Josette. He was always taking refuge; during the war he went to Roussillon in the Pays d'Apt. Roussillon where all is red. He and I hid away together. We were anonymous strangers on the run, perched on a hill, working the land, pissing in a barrel of sawdust. Hayden also painted during the war. He painted the landscapes of the Roussillon. Houses, hills, lanes that were red and ochre-coloured – the red of the dead that the war had left weighing on our backs – Hayden painted all of that. He followed the reds into the quarries where the huge reddish deposit of ochre was mined. The red played out in the sand, a monochrome of ochres, and Hayden represented them on canvas. On canvasses he had made with sheets. Made himself, with his own hands. In Roussillon, my hands worked in the fields and in the vineyards. I carried boxes of grapes; I was a writer on a break. I ran after the meat, after a few scrag ends for the carnivore in me. I hardly wrote at all, a few scraps and scribbles in my *carnets*. A break. And then it came back.

Almost without realizing, I took it up again. Laborious pen-pusher, sweating like an ox dragging a cart in the early morning. Ploughing my narrow furrow. I took it up again. In Ussy, I slaved at my desk. It was a cherished place. In Ussy, I plucked the most beautiful feather from my wing. A feather taken from a black swan's plumage.

Go on! Oh drat … Try again, Madame Mélinge. Well done! Five and three, eight and two are ten. It's your turn. Wow! Spot on! Fifty!

Now, for the mini-bowling … Madame Joffrin, you have to get the big ball to slide along the surface – there you go – to knock down all the little skittles at the end of the lane. Good job! Only two left now. Mind where you put your fingers. You have to push the balls and not the little gutter.

The silly geese are cackling. That's the right word. Others honk, bark and hiss. They cackle and gobble. They play chasing the collapsibles in the garden. Collapsible is the right word. I have to admit that I am a voyeur. I stare at them from behind the curtains of my hatchery, from my rear window. Irrepressible scoping impulse. A writer's perversion, an eternal youth, artful voyeur. In the past, I used to observe Suzanne. Suzanne at the piano, sitting next to her pupils, swinging her impatient legs. Suzanne running along the pavements in Paris, Rue Bernard-Palissy, with my manuscripts in her pockets. A bored Suzanne waiting silently while the deputy mayor wrapped in his scarf made her Madame Beckett.

Suzanne didn't like Ussy all that much – just the garden. She didn't go there very often, only in the beginning. In fine weather, the happy days. Train to Meaux, an hour and ten minutes. Then we would walk the seventeen kilometres to Ussy. Light luggage. It was not unpleasant.

In fine weather the little berries on the ash tree, the red berries, attracted the thrushes, the black-headed warblers and the blue tits. The sparrows flitted around from the chestnut tree to the Manitoba maple tree. They weren't alone; they were beasts among other beasts. A few metres lower down, the blasted troupe of *talpa caeca* – also known as Mediterranean moles – invaded the garden. Each day, the secret society of the grubbers gained new ground underground. They finally set up camp at the foot of my linden tree. Dozens of mole-hills, mounds of humus dredged up from the depths, created an invaders' acropolis in Ussy, in my garden. We tried everything. We hit them with rakes. We whacked them with spades. Nothing doing. *We're in the country*, my neighbour Jean would say. He knew the moles; they were in the fields around his farm. Jean wanted to do things for the best. He wanted to do the best for me. He pulled out all the stops. He used to sit on a folding chair in front of the linden tree with a shotgun in his hand. He waited. He waited for the digging to start. He watched, gun at the ready. But the scratching never started. The scratching never started when Jean was sitting there with his shotgun trained on the target molehill, ears cocked for the least sound of scratching. Jean would come in from the garden empty-handed, folding chair in his arms, shotgun slung across his shoulder. One day he changed tactics – he stuffed the molehills with mothballs, mined them with little white balls. They smelled strongly but the moles didn't bite. No victim in sight. Another failure. Jean didn't surrender – he continued to wage his merciless war. He got new ammunition at the co-op stores. He stuffed deadly poison into some worms, an amuse-bouche for moles. The blind moles were oblivious to the danger – their view of the world mediated by their stomachs. He filled all the holes. The moles feasted and gorged themselves. The sin of gluttony. A mortal sin. End game for the moles.

In fine weather, from time to time, Suzanne would get the urge to go out into the garden, to breathe in the fresh air and offer up her breasts to the sun. Suzanne would step carefully over the molehills, with a rattan chaise longue in her hands and a black-ribbon-bedecked boater on her head. Once settled, she would cast off her clothes and begin a long siesta dressed only in her birthday suit. Her nipples turned golden and sometimes roasted. I observed her from the window of my study, like a discreet satyr. I also watched the oglers, the virgin youths of Molien who looked at her browning in the sun over the wall. I could see them. I could see the tops of their heads over the wall, their leering gazes; the moustache-less mugs to whom I had handed out sweets the previous day. They feasted on Suzanne goggle-eyed, followed the shifts in her position. Lying on her stomach, then on her back. A rotation every quarter of an hour. Suzanne brought them pleasure. Every quarter of an hour.

*

Mr Beckett? This is Maître Fauvette on the line. Right, I've prepared all the documents for the file on the house in Ussy. I spoke to your friends Jean and Nicole on the phone yesterday. I explained everything to them. I also spoke to your nephews. Everyone agrees, nothing to report. Can we meet as planned tomorrow? 2.30 pm at the PLM Hotel, 17 Boulevard Saint-Jacques?

Nicole and Jean here in Paris, on the Boulevard Saint-Jacques. Oh joy. Nicole, Jean, and all of Ussy in their wake. In their baggage. In the trailer behind the van. In the soft earth caught in the grooves of the crushing wheels. Remains of the happy days when the plains of Ussy were mine to walk.

The plains: *not too green, not too flat*. A humble land. The road to Molien, the orchard road that led to the pigeon house on the old farm, and at the end of the road was a dead end, a cul-de-sac. A cul-de-sac where a giant lived. Hyperbole. 'The Giant', that's what he was called in Ussy and elsewhere also, I think: 'André the Giant'. Nicole called him 'Dédé the Dice'. I didn't know him. Just vaguely. Sometimes I would run into himself and his brothers and sisters on the way to school. Or later, I'd see him in the café seated at the counter with its blue rug and its tray of dice. I knew him to see. A bent figure standing next to his father, sawing wood on winter Sundays before the snow covered Ussy. Before the layer of particles of ramified and crystallized ice muffled the noises of the village. Before all the colours were buried beneath a cotton-wool membrane, which stuck to Issy like a second skin, for the months with an 'r', as Jean used to say. These days, Dédé is a wrestler, apparently. A champion, even in Japan. Ussy, the fertile land of myths, and the cradle of giants.

One day big Dédé broke the seat on the tractor. The black seat made of polyvinyl chloride. It collapsed under the weight of the giant's frame. Off to the scrapyard. Knocked out. Dédé the colossus couldn't get into a car. Unless he was bent over and his head was sticking out of the roof that someone had opened so he could get inside. The roof of the 2CV rolled back, Dédé's head in the wind in Ussy as if he were at sea. Captain Dédé was squeezed into the back seat. Huddled up, with his legs sticking out through the windows, hanging over the edge of the doors. Dédé slicing the air with his shanks as thick as masts. Dédé the man-ship.

Old Alphonsine also drove on the roads of Ussy. Alphonsine was Jean's grandmother – 'Granny Fonsie'. She drove a child's pushchair, a small rusty white wrought-iron carriage, a relic of the past. Wrapped up in her shawl, she pushed her precious carriage in all weathers. The baby carriage was not covered – it was a convertible. An open-air pram. What had happened to the hood? This was an impenetrable mystery. Had Fonsie removed it to make the carriage, in which she used to store her shopping, more accessible? Had it simply succumbed to the onslaught of moths? Had a gust of wind swept it away one evening, just as the buds on the maple trees hinted at the arrival of milder weather? Perhaps. Unless the disappearance of the cover was the result of a dreadful theft. A theft from poor Fonsie, whose wobbly balance depended on the indispensable pushchair. Or perhaps there had never ever been a hood on the vehicle? It's possible. In any case, Granny Fonsie leaned on the curved bar of the baby carriage as if it were a walking stick. It created a form of kinetic energy; driven by its own weight. Energy equal to the work of the forces

applied to move the body from being at rest to being in movement. Fonsie was driving the pram that was driving her. The
four large wheels squeaked rhythmically as she passed. I could
hear her coming from a distance. The wheels squeaked as her
shuffling footsteps beat out the after beat. It was a slow jazz
tune. Fonsie's jazz as she went shopping and came to do my
cleaning. Not many off-beat moments. I could count on her.

Jean and his wife Nicole used to call her 'Granny', in
country fashion. I called her 'Madame'. 'Madame Alphonsine'.
That was what my mother had taught me, I used a deferen-
tial courteous tone, without being familiar. No scrimping on
good manners. It was a form of Protestant warmth, a ten-de-
gree drop in temperature. I think Fonsie liked it. She liked it
when I called her 'Madame' or 'Madame Alphonsine', when I
paid her corolla of white hair the tributes it deserved. I was
polite – 'for an Irishman' – which made up a little for the
reservations I knew she had, despite her silence, not about
my origins per se, but about my drinking – a more-or-less
direct corollary. Although Fonsie's reservations were hidden,
I could feel them. I could feel them when she glanced at the
doorway and gazed fixedly at her baby carriage, in which
empty Jameson bottles were piled up with other bags of
rubbish on the days she went 'to the dump'. Fonsie would
then walk back along the road past the school to the end of
the driveway, to the bottle bank. The containers resembled
closed-in urinals – both in their colour and in the way the
young people used them on their nights out on the town.
I imagined Fonsie counting each bottle, taking stock of the
dead soldiers she was sliding into the black rubber slot, the
combination of effluents rising to her nostrils and turning

her stomach. I could see her quietly cursing and swearing, pouring out the bad thoughts she hid in my presence. Thoughts she kept to herself and shared with no one. Low litanies of blasphemy. Silent reproaches. Cathartic rituals.

When she thought she was alone, May swore at the whole world. She cursed like a trooper. Used an assortment of flowery epithets – of which the English language has no shortage – we like to replace them on the page with one or more asterisks depending on the level of vulgarity attained. Let's carry out an objective assessment. It seems to me that the linguistic fantasies involving the Almighty, his son and his saints are greatly overrated. By this I mean that 'damn', 'bloody', 'oh my God' should not, in my view, figure at the top of the list of insults in an age when crucifix-eaters struggle to clear the dust that collects on church pews, including in Ireland. Who can they still offend with their gibes dropped at the beginning or end of a sentence, like farts on oilcloth? A reflex action or a necessity, I wonder? I've always had a preference for saucy insults – I'm not sure if that's the right word. Let's say insults of a more or less pornographic nature. Whatever the nature or eccentricity of the sexual practice evoked. This is certainly out of fashion nowadays or distress-ingly commonplace. In old Ireland, it caused a stir. All you had to do was start a phrase with a straightforward F-word, force-fully stated, for it to have a little effect. I exhibited no restraint. Whenever the opportunity arose, on the streets, in the pubs, I would whistle an F-word, with my lips pursed and my teeth bared. I got into a few scrapes for it, by the way. But whatever the consequences, I must say that I always pronounced the F-word with a certain degree of pleasure. Perhaps because I loved danger. Or out of pure masochism. I spat out my verbal bullets without worrying about the fierce fury that my invective had provoked. Without the slightest regret.

May never did that. Even when she was alone and given to outbursts of mind-boggling profanity – by the standards of anyone who knew May – she never did that. She didn't use the F-word, as we said in my house. As the Puritans say. She much preferred Christ and his apostles, the first category, mentioned earlier. The nice insults that we had always been forbidden to use, and that we were told would make those who dared to say them or even think them burn in hell. These were the blasphemies she purged herself of when she was alone. It was a form of salutary cleansing that happened when she believed that the only witnesses to her sins were the echo of the empty kitchen and the God in question, who was her main concern. If she had known – if she had even suspected – that those words, uttered in violent solitary fits, had reached my ears – on the evenings when I spied on her from the top of the stairs, with my child's head slipped through the wooden bars – she would have died. Anyway, May is dead. At peace, at last. Let's not talk about it any more.

On certain days, Alphonsine also carried eggs in her baby carriage – a homemade walker, a clever recycling of the ornaments of motherhood – eggs that were still covered in feathers. Eggs from her home, laid in the coop in her garden. Eggs from the day before – 'eggs laid the same day still have the germs from the chickens,' she said. Alphonsine's eggs coagulated perfectly and there were no nasty surprises. I swallowed them enthusiastically. Soft, poached, scrambled and even raw – those mornings after Jameson's.

When she couldn't do for me any longer, when the baby carriage was no longer enough to keep Alphonsine upright like other bipeds, she sent me Nicole – Jean's wife. Her grandson's wife. Nicole, three times younger than Alphonsine, three times a mother, three times nicer than the average person. Nicole was discreet. She knew my habits – there were to be no visits while I worked. She complied gracefully with the rules I imposed on her – my neurotic rules – with the air of a soldier who gave me her full allegiance. I was shamefully grateful. Grateful that she was prepared to make the best of things. That she put up with my obscene fussiness, tolerated my compulsive old bachelor rituals, accepted my poor self. It was a challenge. In the course of my life, it seems to me that few people have managed to put up with me. I mean, to put up with me in a way that I can bear. It must be said that I don't put up with much. Not the railway workers' strike, nor chit-chat, nor the pain of my leg hanging in the air as the physio insists I maintain it. I can't stand much of anything. Inapt for the world. An instinct for solitude.

I would always let Nicole know when I was coming. One phone call and the house was ready. Even before the train pulled into the station. Before I got into the grey 2CV with its quilted canvas roof that was faithfully waiting for me in front of the arches. Before I turned the key in the door of the house that always welcomed my solitude with open arms. My house in Ussy.

Mr Beckett? Maître Fauvette here. Are we still meeting tomorrow? Would you like me to pick you up before the meeting and we can go to the PLM together?

Funny old bird, that solicitor. Rather nice, if truth be told. No, tomorrow my walking stick will take me to Boulevard Saint-Jacques. It knows the way. The cane I will drag along and it will drag me after it, along Rue Rémy Dumoncel, Rue Dareau and Boulevard Saint-Jacques. We'll drag our three skinny legs along the pavement, to number seventeen. To the hotel built on a quarry that used to be called 'The Lion's Den'. A pit in which all sorts of ferocious beasts used to kill each other, it seems: schoolchildren from suburban boarding schools, acrobats, thread-eaters, sword-swallowers, exhibitors of polyglot dwarfs. A great human circus like no other. Although … as I take a closer look … through my window or in the mirror … we are no better.

Le Tiers-Temps, Residence for Senior Citizens, Paris

13 August 1989

Sunday, five o'clock, an impromptu visit from the publisher-to-whom-I-owe-everything, while a young hairdresser is combing my stubborn locks. Caught in the act of pruning. The hairdresser not only cuts my hair – which he does, catching my hair in small clumps between his index and middle fingers to straighten it out – he also comments on each gesture he makes; he is in high spirits on this late summer afternoon.

'Look,' he says, 'you have amazing hair for your age, Mr Beckett. I've never seen anything like it! I'm going to thin it out a bit, on top, so that it doesn't fluff out so much.'

Less fluffy, I'm not sure about that. My level of annoyance was already relatively high at the beginning of the grooming session. The young hairdresser, who was visibly happy with his expertise, thought it wise to add these few words, which sounded like a promise: 'You'll see, you'll be happy, you'll be able to fix your hair in a jiffy.'

Why is it that even in old age, in the winter of man's existence – the winter of his discontent – a man who no longer aspires to anything but a little peace, is confronted, in spite of himself, with so much stupidity? I mean, how is it that an old man – as soon as he is forced to associate with a cohort he did everything to avoid up until now (medical staff, barbers, etc.) – becomes a pet in front of which people start gabbing? In that respect he is not so different from a poodle, the old man entrusted with people's unimportant views on things. He becomes a receptacle for the dregs of language and thought. A victim of everyone's nonsense and, what's more, it happens in front of witnesses. Yet another privilege.

The Publisher, my publisher, my most faithful of faithful friends, came up to me as casually as possible, pretending not to be in any way disconcerted by my position, which, when he entered the room, was as follows: head back, abandoned as if on the scaffold in the hands of the barber, gazing at the ceiling, with the rest of my body draped in a black smock like the high priest in Tullow church during service.

Then an incredibly old-fashioned phrase occurred to me, which seemed appropriate at the time: 'Finish coming in.'

A priceless expression. Apparently it comes from the Occitan language. 'Finissez d'entrer,' as if the action of crossing the threshold by a few centimetres required a succession of stages at the end of which it was necessary to issue another invitation so as to reach the final, glorious crossing of the aforementioned threshold. Anyway, my publisher friend successfully finished entering, put the bottle of whiskey he had in his hands on the table and sat down in the front row to see the live show I was part of, against my better judgment – the pitiful spectacle of an old male being shorn of his mane. Its removal was necessary. A form of inevitable castration. *Honni soit qui mal y pousse*, I thought. Well, that's quite hard to say. *Honni soit qui mal y pousse*. The famous French fricative consonants, the glottis allowing air to pass through it with a rubbing motion. At home, we tended to stammer occlusives, the complete closure of the mouth followed by an abrupt opening. Guaranteed plosives to follow: Peter Piper picked a peck of pickled peppers.

I resolved to share this thought aloud: *Honni soit qui mal y pousse*. Covering my embarrassment with words. Using my wit to sweep aside my embarrassment at being reduced to the rank of the common herd shorn in front of a crowd – remember, I was on the right side during the war. So I spoke out loud, convinced that I would win everyone's approval: '*Honni soit qui mal y pousse!*' I said. 'Cursed be the things that grow badly and stick up.'

Running his right hand over his bare head, the publisher-to-whom-I-owe-everything replied in a mocking tone: 'Hirsutism is a problem I don't have.'

How could I not have thought of that? How could I have forgotten the large bald forehead – a distinctive characteristic of the Publisher, together with his piercing eagle eyes and his broad smile. How could I have made the consonants whistle without putting myself in the shoes of this other man, who had always put himself in mine so well. Who had always read me so well. Who had read my work so well. This episode is unfortunately emblematic of what happens when I open my mouth even the slightest bit, whether my glottis is tight or not. Ah, the art of conversation was a gift the fairies failed to grant me, if they ever leaned over my cradle. A cradle from which I have kept falling, it seems. Perhaps that's it. I was left crippled. Crippled by conversation. By chatter between my fellow human beings. Silence is followed by blunders. An average of three or four stupid things per hour on a good day. If only I could keep quiet, as I know I should. But I persist. I forget. I relapse. I'm not even talking about the hours when I am slightly tipsy and give up any form of vigilance. After the second drink, the average goes back up. And the phenomenon intensifies until it is multiplied by three. A disaster. In the event of a complete and utter bender, it becomes cataclysmic, unstoppable. Hurricanes of bullshit rain down on my fellow human beings without my even realizing it. Leaving me contrite, the next day. Determined to keep my mouth shut until the next recurrence. Speech is a curse. No, I don't say anything worthwhile. In writing, perhaps. If at all.

Luckily, my publisher friend – the safest and wisest friend there is – has no need to speak. He doesn't need to speak to me, to ask me what I am doing. His eyes tell him that I am doing nothing. That I can do nothing more. That I am lying there inert. Condemned to imagine what I might write, if I were still writing. That I am there, scratching unreadable letters on the slate of my floating thoughts. Words that come out in dribs and drabs. That are almost erased. He doesn't need to ask; he knows that I'm just waiting. Waiting for it to finally fade away.

The Publisher is magnificently silent. Masterfully silent, I would even say. Eloquently silent. A virtuoso of silence, he remains silent and rolls his eyeballs like a frightened horse. His magnificent eyes probe both the whole and its detail: old Sam, in his priest's smock, the barber with his trousers at half-mast – builder's bum. And I enjoy his silence. The silence he allows himself without embarrassment. The silence of a man who deciphers things, who understands everything, who says everything without indiscretion.

The barber finally fell silent, in response to the unbearable racket of the cursed hairdryer. He put away the black overall. The barber's scene has come to an end. *Cut!* The boy leaves. The editor friend opens the bottle. *A pause*. We drink. Together. In silence.

Le Tiers-Temps, Residence for Senior Citizens, Paris
14 August 1989

Last night my neighbour's screams brought me out of my room. Out of the room I rarely leave. I was sitting at my table. I am often at my table. I was looking for a word. *Starts*. The word came to me and I wrote it down. I wrote *starts*, or rather, I was still writing *starts* next to my title, *Stirrings Still* – I'm so slow – when the convulsive starts, the real ones, those of my neighbour, started. Starts that I could hear without seeing them, in the modulations of my neighbour's voice, which screamed until it rasped at the back of her throat. It scraped the ears in the walls. There were muffled screams. The cries of a creature whose bruised flesh is flayed one last time before giving up. Before giving in to the end that is hers, before giving back her last words, her last sounds – her final legacy.

What did she say? What did my neighbour say? The elderly woman next door whose very existence resounds as if she were there in my room. At my side. The walls are very thin. The lack of privacy in old age where we constantly hear the unfamiliar others, the acute problem of the constant soundscape – from the moment when night joins day to the time when it disappears. The lack of privacy and the echoes of other old people – from the rattle of the morning to the coughing in the evening, including her little prayers. The little prayers did her good. They reassured my neighbour, my next-door neighbour. I could hear her reciting a prayer in a low voice; it was always the same one, which was as foreign to me as she was. An evening prayer. It went like this:

Je Vous adore, oh mon Dieu, with the submission inspired by the presence of Your sovereign greatness.
I believe in You; *vous êtes la vérité même;*
I believe in You because You are infinitely good;
Je Vous aime with all my heart because You are eminently lovable and I love my neighbour as myself for love of You.

Well, I care as much about God as I do about Bonaparte's first sock. He means as much to me as my first jibe or my first dose of the clap – dirty old man – but I must say that initially I was a little amused. It amused me to hear the recitation of my imposed companion. I was forced on her, as she was on me, an arranged marriage through the walls – it reminded me of boarding school. My prankster days. Portora Royal School in County Fermanagh, a Protestant institution several centuries old, was where I spent my youth. The sound reminded me of the dormitories. The mumbling, the stories of Conan Doyle and Sherlock Holmes whispered at night. It wasn't unpleasant. Living together, on either side of the wall.

We got on well. We got close to each other, literally. In fact, night after night, I began to listen and know the prayer so well that I could have recited it by heart, had I been asked. I wasn't asked. But I could have. It has to be said, although I'm an unrepentant atheist – and it's strange that I am as much of an atheist as I am, but that's the way it is – I thought the prayer was pretty. I'm referring to the style. It was old style, a grand old style. I don't care for it any more of course, but in the prayer genre, I thought it was pretty good. Your sovereign greatness, that's something. And I could hear her properly, because her bed – she's ninety-nine and the doyenne of Le Tiers-Temps, according to Nadja the nurse – was stuck against the wall. The head of her bed against mine, if you like, but on the other side. That's why I could hear her so well. I could even hear her asides. The moments when she spoke to herself, to encourage herself. When she was her own audience. Did she know that I could hear her as she could certainly hear me? That I was the voyeur of her torments? I was an obscene witness, on the other side of the wall. I'm not sure.

But tonight, last night, as I wrote at my table, there was no evening prayer, no submission to the sovereign greatness of the Most High. Instead, my next-door neighbour screamed with all the strength that her end would allow. Low cries. Exhausted exhaling cries. What did she say? A man's name. Perhaps a husband, a father or a brother. Unless it was her true love, lost so long ago. Her first love for a modest man. He was not welcome. In the family, the modest but true loves were never welcome. She didn't choose. She didn't choose him. The modest man left. Yet that night, in her room, with her last breath before she died, she called out his name as if he were coming. As if he were already there, before her eyes. Her lost love, returned just in time, before the light became meaningless. You are delirious, my poor old man. You are rewriting the ending. You can't help it. Nobody knows what she meant. Nobody knows the end.

What I do know is that when that name resonated on her purple lips, a name unknown to me, I was still writing at my table. I could give the time to the police, if they came. Or to the clerk at the town hall. I could tell him, *It was around eight o'clock at night,* at the time when I am still writing at my table, that was when the doyenne gave her last cry. As I was caught up in my *soubresauts,* my starts and jolts, I heard hers. Perhaps the officer will ask me about that moment. About the moment, about her last cry. About the moment of the last moment. Perhaps he will question me.

Mr Beckett, what were you doing at the time you heard the screams?

I was writing.

Writing? Do you still write?

Not really.

Then why do you say you were writing?

...

What were you doing when your neighbour died?

I was writing.

You were writing, you say. So you still write?

Inept words from the duty sergeant – a new nightmare – while the doyenne is still lying in the adjoining room. Not yet cold. I resign myself to silence. My sole consolation. Silence.

Sir, what did you do when you heard her scream?

I got up, as soon as I could – I am so slow. I got up, clung on to the table. The table I write on. I shouted back, into the corridors, waking the duty staff. My hoarse voice sounded the alarm, relaying the knell that my neighbour had undertaken to sound herself. With all her might. Not loud enough. I shouted for her. It was a crescendo of disjointed words. An angry roar. It seemed to me that my voice tore through the night, that it relayed my neighbour's voice. Redoubling her cries, her cries of love lost and found. When my legs reached the room next to mine – also on the ground floor, but with no view of the garden – when my trembling hands knocked on the door, turned the handle, the end was in sight. Swarms of nurses flew to her bedside. Their blue scrubs made a sky around the bed. It was an electric bed and the old woman had pressed the button to raise herself up. To face up to death. Stiff with pain, her eyes were sunk into the empty sockets of death. My neighbour's blue eyes were full of agony and terror. It was a terrifying vision. There was no happy end. Her final suffering, her last fears and the only remedy offered was the feigned affection of the staff. For those who are experienced in the dominion of death and have learned the words and gestures of circumstance. They are weak palliatives. My neighbour is dead. There will be no more little prayers. I can no longer hear her. I can only hear myself. And the silence.

*

The solicitor said half past two. It's written down in my notebook. A brown Moleskine notebook with a black flap where I write everything down in my old cat's scrawl. See you at half past two this very afternoon. My neighbour's death was unforeseen – it's not in the notebook. This afternoon, for a little while, I will leave behind me the place and the death that lurks there. For a few stolen hours. An appointment with the solicitor, what a strange coincidence that it should happen today. An appointment with the solicitor, when death has just struck. Not me, but my neighbour. Just next door. I felt the wind of the cannonball pass me by. A hair's breadth away. Brushing against my temples. Just as I felt it brush past me once and still miss me. It's always close, always next door. At half past two, it will not be about the neighbour, nor about her death, but about what will happen to the house in Ussy when I am no more. *When I am no more* – what a dramatic tone. I am already unable to go to my house in Ussy where I spent so much time. Unable to get into the 2CV whose grey hood has faded in the sun. Nicole said it faded in the moon. She said that the car, which slept outside, at nightfall, was *struck by the moonlight* and it burnt the canvas top. The canvas top that served as the roof to my grey 2CV. The canvas was perforated by the stars and the weather, which allowed the air to pass through like a breath of freedom pushing me towards the house. The house that held out its arms to me. With my grey 2CV, I drove like the blazes. All the way to Ussy. Right into the garden where I made the car skid to a halt. Like a child. I unlocked the door of the white house with one turn of the key – the white house! Like a child. I put my shoes inside the trunk in the entrance hall and opened the sliding doors. There, in the living room, as they say in the country, in the room where everything happens, where everything can happen. I sat down at my desk. It was a moment of grace.

Like everything else, my desk was rather spartan. Dark wood. Four drawers. One typewriter. I always kept a white packet of cigarillos on the left-hand side, with a portrait of a marquise or diplomat on it – political smokes. An ashtray on the right-hand side – for convenience. An ashtray with a steel push-button and rotating lid – I won it in a raffle in Ussy. *Well aren't you lucky*, Nicole said. One push with my index finger and the ashes and cigarette butts disappeared. In no time, with sleight of hand. I smoked with my hands free, sucking on the butt that was stuck to my lips. The smoke came out of my nostrils, making me disappear into a cloud of fog, until the stub ended up in the ashtray. One push with my index finger. One rotation. Nothing left.

From the desk – my observation post – I could see into the garden. The outside came to me. Old landscapes encountered in dreams, landscapes imagined by others, combined with those I could admire through the window. There were two men, two comrades contemplating the vaporous moon at the foot of an uprooted tree. The image came to me. The leaning tree that had not yet fallen. The tree that had lived long enough to feel a hundred years old, and that halfway to falling seemed to dance. It came to me. Two men were also leaning at the foot of a tree and there was a huge stone. It was a dolmen – a mysterious megalith, such as one found under the hooves of the first Irish horses. I drew my inspiration from it. I let the lights of the night come to me, the lights of the countryside in the fog, which, little by little, became invisible. It was a place of wandering. I couldn't see much. I could just make out the silhouettes of the two comrades as they stood up and sat down again, their hats bobbing on their heads in the dark. The blackness of my thoughts, and of the ink my machine was putting on the dialogues my fingers were typing. My dialogues were cracked. My characters were too.

What else was there in the living room? I remember the boat bed that we used to sit on; Hayden used to sit on it and I used to serve him drinks – during the endless games that we played out on my grandfather's chessboard. The kitchen was at the end of the hall. In the evening, we would sneak back and forth to replenish glasses. The corridor too became endless, until we reached the kitchen – a place for storage. The kitchen was rudimentary: a sink, a table covered with a fuchsia tablecloth cut from a modern fabric. Not an oilcloth, a coated cotton cloth, down which ran a river of café au lait when I clumsily dropped my bowl in the morning. I often dropped it, I'm not an early riser. Suzanne knew this. That's why she bought the modern tablecloth. So that the liquid would run. So it wouldn't stain. As for the fuchsia, I never knew why. Why fuchsia pink? Maybe to brighten up the room, which was as austere as a convent kitchen, with its wicker chairs and rickety table. I almost forgot about the *vide-poches* – that essential kitchen object. That small dish which, when left on the tablecloth, was so useful for relaying messages for Nicole.

Thank you so much for the delicious vegetables from the garden and for the house, like a new penny! Speaking of pennies, here are three for the kids' piggy banks.
Give them a kiss for me.

Sam Beckett

I felt compelled to write 'Beckett'. It's silly, but I felt compelled to write it for one simple reason: Nicole always called me 'Mr Beckett'. I didn't really like it. It sounded a bit bossy. A bit superior. Especially since I, as she was younger, called her Nicole. I didn't really like it. That old-school side: me, 'Sir', and her, 'Nicole'. But I couldn't tell her to call me Sam either. Knowing the French, who are very keen on 'Monsieur Madame', it would have sounded a bit cavalier. That wasn't the point. Incidentally, the French have always made me laugh with their good manners. With their grand formulas. A sense of solemnity which, for them, is not at all incompatible with the fact of sleeping with the aforementioned 'Madame' – the neighbour across the street or the wife of their best friend, for example. 'Madame' prevents nothing, quite the contrary in fact. 'Madame' opens the gates to a paradise of boundless courtesy. *Madame, let me put the flowers on your bodice straight.* French politeness if ever there was one. At the very least. And I must say that in this respect I feel very patriotic. French by adoption, I might add. *My respects, Madame.* You poor thing.

'Mr Beckett, you haven't touched your lunch tray! It's good today though, look: three-fish terrine; roast beef, duchess potatoes and carrots; cheese; morello cherry pie. I'll give you a little more time. I'll pick up your tray last.'

Not hungry. No appetite. And I doubt if her presence will help me at all. The presence of the kindly fat lady. Not an attractive view. So let her take back her tray, opulent bosom dipping into gravy and duchess potatoes. Quite an agenda. You cantankerous old man. You are still shaken by your night. Your night of terror. You'll be late. You've got to get your skates on and head for the PLM Saint-Jacques hotel –

a marathon trip with your cane. The most modern hotel in the world, with its flaky facade and high-speed lifts. Nicole and Jean will never get over it. You won't be able to get back to Ussy. In a few hours it will be over – the house, the garden. Case closed. No more pleasure any more. You can't have it any more. You've had enough.

Le Tiers-Temps, Residence for Senior Citizens, Paris

20 August 1989

[Radio]

Hello everyone, this evening the programme Les Archives du théâtre *will allow listeners to follow in the footsteps of Samuel Beckett, the most French of Irishmen, a master of language and the absurd. This year, the writer and playwright celebrates the twentieth anniversary of a Nobel Prize that he refused to collect in person – because he was too shy, according to some people, because he wanted to provoke, according to others. Nonetheless, this anniversary gives us the opportunity to allow you to explore the hidden treasures of the theatre archives. In a few moments we will play an interview with the actor Vittorio Caprioli, broadcast when* Aspettando Godot *was first performed in Italy. This archive will be followed by a full broadcast of the play, in French, directed – as it was originally in 1953 – by the great Roger Blin for the Comédie-Française on 2 April 1978.*

Three, two, one, zero … Allô Paris, ici Rome. *Theatrical consolations are assembled, dispersed and remade again, according to the moods of the artists, the demands of the impresarios and the whims of the cinema. The director Luciano Mondolfo and the actor Vittorio Caprioli found themselves on the stage of a small elegant Roman theatre, the theatre at 6 Via Vittoria. They combined their talent with that of Marcello Moretti, who had, you will remember, achieved great success in Paris as Harlequin in Goldoni's play* The Servant of Two Masters, *produced by the Piccolo Teatro. Together with Claudio Ermelli, Antonio Pierfederici, Caprioli and Moretti, they have been performing an Italian version of Samuel Beckett's* Waiting for Godot *for several weeks now with great success. The painter Giulio Coltellacci has created a strikingly simple and tragically sober set. The assembled intelligentsia of Rome has been attending the show. Monsieur Caprioli, may I offer you my congratulations, and I would also like to congratulate myself for being able to interview you for this special programme …*

Let them congratulate themselves if it pleases them! The plea-sure is all mine. The pleasure was all mine. Thanks to Suzanne – to whom I owe a debt of eternal gratitude. Suzanne, who took the lead when I was left behind, peddling plays, selling manuscripts. Who waited in the rain, her hands weighed down with pages. Who knocked on all the doors, climbed the echoing staircases of the big publishing houses and theatres. Suzanne the spy in the *conciergeries* and theatres, lurking in the shadow of the master who was not a master. The master of language who had put his own in his pocket. Swallowed it. The fearful master who held his tongue. For fear it would fall out. For fear it would slip. Or who, in desperation, gave it to the cat – the cat got my tongue. Master Coward in his hidden bolthole. The pleasure was all mine and it was down to Suzanne. A pleasure built from scratch. Built by her hands, for each play. A theatrical puzzle built by Suzanne, while I stood by, scribbling. I wrote while *Waiting* for it to happen. Waiting for it to be done. Suzanne took the bull by the horns. Disregarding my infidelities. She screwed her courage to the sticking place with both hands, with the courage that I was missing. I miss Suzanne. Courage still missing.

Suzanne saw them all. The Lindons, the Blins – the ones who pulled me out of the hole I had dug myself into. Not an unpleasant hole, by the way. In any case, I had got used to it without trying very hard. Without it feeling like a hole, I mean like a crack or a tear in the surface. No, my hole, or rather the hole I was in when I was taken out, was more like a bolthole. A bolthole in which I enjoyed writing. In which I could finally write to my heart's content. Without worrying about the rest. About the remains of the world above me. In my hole, I was buried up to the waist, but my hands were free to frantically blacken the pages. The valves were open. My plume floated free, like a pigeon, a migratory bird, which when injured is forced to interrupt its journey. When its wing is healed, it then decides to spread its wings and flap to the point of exhaustion. Until the ecstasy of the flight makes it fall limply onto the first branch. Unless a cartridge interrupts its flight. A tragic end. It was not mine.

If truth be told, in my hole – the hole I had scratched out for myself and in which I was scribbling – I was perhaps not *happy*, but I was relieved. Yes, relieved. Scratching offers relief. At least there and then. I was all the more relieved because the accumulation that had gone on for too long before the scratching period had had the effect of forming a sort of abscess that made me suffer and the scratching had relieved it. The pleasure of the patient. A small pleasure. A flood of pus had followed. The pus pissed like rain. A half-life that went by in less time than it takes to say it. Than it takes to say it all. Than it takes to write it. I was busy with my escape. With my boots on my feet. Trying to empty the hole as it filled up with the half-life that was coming back to confront me. Which was coming back to me. A life I had to let go of. I had to deliver in pain. The attentive ear – the one I always imagined behind me when I was writing – was at my side. In the hole. At my side, among the countless characters, the unnamable ones for whom I still had to find a name. The names came all at once: Molloy, Estragon, Vladimir, Malone. They came. They all came. And what's more, the hole was full. Like a fresh egg from the day before.

[Radio]

Dear listeners, when the play was premiered one newspaper critic wondered about the wait for the famous Godot. The waiting is the real topic of the play and behind it is the myth conjured up by the author of an ideal, which each of us hankers after and never reaches, an ideal which gives us the strength to continue with our lives. Samuel Beckett represents the existence of the poor unfortunates, in other words, ourselves with a cruelty that is the equal of Pozzo's cruelty to his slave, who has a rope tied around his neck as a symbol of man's exploitation of his fellow man.

Another critic found fault with the play, and with Roger Blin's direction, saying that the work is difficult for the general public. Nevertheless, while Waiting for Godot *is no doubt a demanding work, which tests the limits of what is bearable, it is precisely because it has planted its tree on this demarcation line that the dramatist goes beyond time and consciousness in a way that would no doubt have enchanted Antonin Artaud.*

The critics' cackle ... The poor unfortunates have taken great pains. And what about my publisher friend? And Blin, the stage director, and the others? They went to so much trouble for a play in which nothing much happened. Where nothing was happening, so to speak. Except perhaps in the mind of the lady in blue in the third row. The one who, faced with the ennui of the sinister scenery (the country road, the tree, the big rock), started to think. Or rather found herself in a pensive mood – a better word, that alludes to the idea of daydreaming. What could she be thinking about anyway? I often thought of her when I imagined a performance of the play – of *Godot* not yet performed, not yet *Godot*. I always imagined, in the third row, the lady in blue who was bored to death and began to think. A remedy for boredom. In the meantime, I mean in the meantime, while *Waiting* for the play to be performed, what was she thinking about? Perhaps about the salesman who came to see her earlier that day, around two o'clock, when she was alone and the emptiness of the house resounded painfully within her. A salesman, pretty as a picture, selling language methods rang her doorbell after lunch. *Good morning, Madame, would you like to learn Italian in a few weeks?* he said. She let him in. She was usually so suspicious but she even invited him to have a cup of coffee, which she was not going to drink alone. Not this time.

It's not difficult, Madame. It's a painless method. You just have to follow it. The fifty lessons are accompanied by sound recordings and cartoons. It's very easy to listen to, you'll see. And very easy. In a few weeks you will be able to read Dante in Italian, Madame. Dante – I'm not kidding!

What happened next? Did she give in to temptation, to temptations? The story does not say. What the story does say – the story that came to me so many times in my hole, when I was imagining it – is that the famous lady in blue, in the third row on the left, I mean on the garden side, was busier thinking about her salesman and his beautiful moustache than about the performance that was being played out on stage before her eyes. A scene that was close to her, at least spatially, but which had not managed to hold her attention. Nonetheless, it seemed that the ditch, the one in which Estragon had slept, also kept the lady away. She was collateral damage. And this from the very beginning of the play. A ditch so big that the spirit of the unfortunate lady – or the fortunate lady, I should say, if we consider the hypothesis of the pleasant hours spent that very afternoon in the company of the salesman – had crossed the ditch and begun to wander. A mind that wandered, that wandered so hard and so far that it never came back. No landing. At least not before the end. The end of Godot, which was late coming. No landing. Not even on the first branch of the tree that was leafless on the stage, generously holding out its branches to her.

Ah well, the wanderings of the mind. Not an exact science. I know something about it; my mind was never very well connected with the rest. With my remains. With my body. And vice-versa for that matter: I mean, my body has never been an excellent partner for my mind either. To say the least. My body, that companion of ill fortune. My poor other half. Always ready to do the opposite of what the rest told it to do, in other words I mean my mind this time. I, like my body, am impulsive, never one to dwell too long in the bosom of my family – yet always ready to welcome all kinds of bosoms, provided their owner is generous enough. My body is willing to serve women, in a rather indiscriminate fashion. The only condition is that they stick to what I can put up with. What can I put up with? Scratches, bites – all fine – but no blows. I can't stand them. They make me see red. No, I've never been able to take a beating. Not those given by my teachers, nor those dished out by May, who always denied having given them when she recovered her senses – she often lost the rag. Her mind wandered on the edge of despair. She suffered from her nerves.

As for my mind, I must say that it is unfortunately no more faithful than the rest of me. By this I mean faithful to my will. A tramping mind, a wandering mind – always wandering the paths and the country roads, instead of focusing on what is being said. What is being done. Always a ways behind. So I have never been angry with the lady in blue in the third row, whom I understood to be a kindred spirit when, like the bull jumping the fence, she allowed her mind to go back to the salesman who had thrilled her so. Who had made her come so often – in that beautiful English expression, *Come, sweetheart* – so often that it was not until the thunderous applause in the little Théâtre de Babylone that she came to herself. That her body and soul returned to the play. At least to the theatre. When I say *thunderous*, it's not so much with the intention of crowing at my own success, implying at the same time that the theatre where my play – in this case *Godot* – was performed was full as a tick, but I say it with the intention of describing the scene as accurately as possible. I suffer from congenital perfectionism. For it so happened that the Théâtre de Babylone had great acoustics, and it amplified the noise of the cheers to which I am very sensitive. Yes, since childhood I have been excessively sensitive to noise – another congenital defect. The noise was all the more difficult to bear for anyone with sensitive ears like mine because the audience that evening was larger than expected, which prompted the staff to add folding chairs in a hurry. Hence the aforementioned thunderous applause, which leads me to crow like a cock who is happy that it's raining thus in his barnyard. Like a cock. I must say that the word cock, *coq* in French, is an eminently suitable term, since in my language this bird can, depending on the context, also refer to the member used a few hours before the play by the salesman to please the lady in blue. Why are you talking about a cock, you old capon!

I wanted to talk about the audience. I imagined the audience to be happy too. Happy that the play was over. One is always happy when everything is over. It is an unquestionable deliverance. Even in the theatre. No matter how good the play. So I was happy to have offered the audience, even after the play, a moment of fleeting happiness. That of the finished play. And when I say spectators, I mean the small handful of those who, with alert cortexes, had waited patiently to discover the secret of the damned Godot. Who waited for an apparition that had not come. That had not come to me. I couldn't help it. The wish to sidestep it was stronger than I knew.

The damned Godot. If Godot exists, I mean in the theatre. It is by the grace of Lord Blin who moved heaven and earth. Blin was more religious than me. That's not hard. He went to so much trouble. They all went to so much trouble. Suzanne, Blin, the Publisher. For Sam the slave-driver. The potential Pozzo. The one who waited and twiddled his thumbs. Waited for others to turn his pages. Suzanne handed them out. Hundreds of pages sent out – messages in bottles. Almost all of them failed to come ashore. A few survived. Washed up by chance in the Publisher's lap.

The Publisher in the metro, La Motte-Picquet–Grenelle station, the manuscript of *Molloy* in his lap. Molloy was talking to the Publisher. He made him laugh. He made him laugh so much that the Publisher laughed like a wrench wheel unscrewing – *like a drain*, as they say where I'm from, another expression we owe to the British, for God's sake. Like a hunchback – with a form of sardonic laughter, an involuntary contraction of the muscles of the face. He laughed so hard he nearly popped the buttons in his waistcoat. He was laughing so hard, he told me, that the manuscript was slipping. He closed it again for fear it would fall. For fear the pages would scatter, a fragile manuscript only just rescued and not yet bound. The Publisher changed onto line 10 and went as far as Sèvres-Babylone. Unless he got off at Odéon, which is possible; the Publisher is a walker. He snuck in, walked through the dirty corridors. The commuters, those who like him were going to their connections, scrutinized the smirk on his face. A trace of the laughter that the madman from *Molloy* had unleashed. The Publisher in the midst of the madmen. In the midst of my madmen. He went to so much trouble so that I would be lucky. Dead lucky.

'Mr Beckett? Sorry to disturb you, but the physio will be here soon.'

In any case my madmen thought of nothing else but that, I mean Vladimir and Estragon. They dreamed of hanging themselves, really hanging themselves. Of dancing in the leaves, a smile on the lips, cock to the sky. Of treating themselves to a good waltz once and for all. Of course the material dimension remained. It was difficult to deal with the technical aspects – the length of the rope, its quality, should it be made out of gut, hemp or jute? If they were lucky enough to have one to hand. Or an equivalent – a piano wire, an electric cable, anything at all would do, if truth be told, anything at all that could have allowed them to swing in the trees one last time, ready to fall.

'She wants to have a look at you and figure out what is up with your legs, what is making walking so difficult.'

But hanging – not the hanging administered as it was in the past by the judges and generously organized by civil servants, no, I mean hanging as it is carried out by ordinary people – is not that easy to accomplish. It demands the capacity to lift oneself up. Unless one calls on an outsider to help, that is.

'Following your request, we have kept her informed of recent developments. She will suggest some exercises.'

In such a situation, as in most other situations, no help is to be obtained from outside sources. Outsiders are no use. Unfortunately, neither am I.

'You see these long white parallel bars? You're going to lean on them; put one under your right hand and one under your left hand like this. And then you're going to walk slowly to the end. The idea is to use your arms as well to relieve the weight on your legs. Above all, take it easy. I'm not timing you. This is not a race, okay? Come on, let's get you set up. Hands ... Very good. Are you ready? Off you go, I'm watching you.'

'...'

'Easy, easy, easy. Easy, Mr Beckett! Why so quick? You're taking too much of a risk! You'll hurt yourself. You think it's funny? What a chancer you are! I know there are mats on the floor but I don't want you to collapse. Come on, let's start again. And take it easy, eh?'

'...'

'Really! Mr Beckett, stop, stop. Wait, wait, wait! Wait, I'm getting you to do this exercise to help you walk better, not to hurt you! Let's give it another shot, but you really need to slow down, okay? Otherwise I'll take you back to your room immediately. I can see that you're enjoying this, but you're in danger of falling. All right. Last try, I'm counting on you to take things easy.'

She as good as scolded me! If I enjoy going fast, I mean on an old man's scale of fast, I'm going to go fast, and that's it. I always go too fast. That's my default setting. I've always loved speed. I am a fiery Aries. A fearless animal. And stubborn as an ox to boot. That's the way it is. I'm incorrigible. Always loved speed. Including when it precipitated my downfall, my loss. Going fast, talking fast. Until I run out of breath. That's what I like. Even in the theatre, like in my play *Not I* – a story told at full speed. A big mouth, ranting and disgusting. A wide mouth, full of teeth. A mouth as beautiful as it is crazy, in theatrical black. Two blood-red lips that go crazy. Ranting. Raving. Roaring. The open mouth of an excited woman. Distraught, I should say. It is the others who are excited by the agitation of a mouth that lets everything out. That holds nothing back. Not even the screams. The mouth of a terrifying woman. I shudder. I often shudder when I see women's mouths. Women who scream. Women who shudder all over and look like the beast whose beauty makes you forget its profound savagery. The sleeping beast, so beautiful that one cannot help but approach it. Unsuspecting. While it sleeps. The charming beast that allows itself to go after devouring its prey. Whose sudden awakening – perhaps it hears a noise, perhaps it's hungry again? – reveals wolf's teeth. This is a nightmare from my childhood. So many nights spent between the teeth of this beautiful mouth. Razor-sharp teeth, guided by the ferocious appetite of a belly that the night prevented me from seeing. Teeth on the edge of a warm caressing tongue. An enveloping irresistible tongue that rubbed carelessly against the cutting edge of the incisors – the cleaver. The nightmare of that mouth in which I found myself, whole or in parts. Always a bit of me in the uncontrollable mouth. The sweet mouth I ventured into at the beginning, without the slightest suspicion. A fearless animal. Young feisty Sam. I moved forward of my own accord, caught up in the warmth of the wet lips and the siren voice that wet the vibrating walls. The wet mouth was a calm sea that washed me with its tongue – it was just rough enough for me – so I surrendered. I was forever surrendering. Until everything trembled. Then a thick fog replaced my thoughts. And gradually the currents changed. Then a warning wave slowly rose up and carried me into the storm. I gave in to the most irrepressible temptation. All of me stretched out towards this mouth that was sucking me in. It sucked me in so uncontrollably that I disappeared entirely inside. I was sucked in by that beautiful mouth. Enveloped by the warm tongue that sucked me to the quick. I tried to get out, like I was Jonah imprisoned in the sucker which, a few minutes earlier, had excited him so much. I was shaking when I woke up, cautiously feeling my body all over. Making sure that nothing was missing. Nothing had disappeared. Had my frenzy caused such confusion that I had lost my way on the narrow border, the dizzying precipice that separates one's nightmares from one's dreams? Had the feeling of surrender, the out-of-body experience, induced by the mouth, revealed fears that were linked to a pleasure which, once spent, would lead to terrible repercussions? I don't know. But what I do know is that sleep has been kind to me each time; time and again, it has welcomed me into those abysses where the terrifying pleasure of an uncontrollable mouth was lodged. I rushed into it every time, driven forward by the gusts of fear that were blowing behind me. What an old masochist I am.

'Mr Beckett, are you all right? You gave me a fright. Thank God for the mats. I told you, you were going too fast. I'll help you up.'

What a beautiful mouth she has. With teeth cut like pearls – and small gaps. When she gets angry, she talks faster. Much faster. Her lips stretch more and more. The corners of her mouth turn up into her cheeks.

'It was too much for our first session. I'm sorry; it's my fault. I'll think of other exercises for next time. More suitable for your leg problems. It was a bad idea to get you to use the bars. It was too soon. I'm sorry.'

Not me. Unexpected sensations. For a time, I thrilled at the delights of danger again; danger, my old friend. I balanced along the ledge. Last dizzy spell before the fall.

Le Tiers-Temps, Residence for Senior Citizens, Paris

25 August 1989

I found a newspaper under my door this morning. The Tiers-Temps newspaper. I've seen it all now, even if I can't see much of anything any more. Its official name is *The Third Age Gazette*. Pinch me, I'm dreaming. It would seem that we owe this brilliant idea to the zeal of a nurse whose name escapes me. I would like to make it clear that, apart from the title, which I will refrain from commenting on as it speaks for itself, the content – if I may be so bold – is intended to relate the painful peregrinations of the silver foxes, those who will be missing in the future. When I say 'missing', I am thinking of those whom we saw not long ago, of whom we had no news and whose name we come across one day engraved on a tombstone when we are out on a walk …

I'm going too fast. I always go too fast. What I wanted to say about the story of this old crock's newspaper. A newspaper for old crocks about to go over to the other side, for those who will be missing in action in the near future – with just a little more effort they're almost there, those old people racing to the exit. Anyway, what I meant to say was that this newspaper thing reminds me of the time when I was trying to throw stones at the bloody seagulls in Merrion Square – pretentious shameless seagulls, one of which had snatched my Cheddar cheese sandwich. I heard a strange dialogue behind me. It was happening on a wooden bench doused with rain, in front of a bed of purple pansies and daffodils in bloom. It was early March, I think. Yet it was so mild that nature itself was deceived into an early blooming. I was throwing stones at the thieving seagulls that were feasting on my lost lunch when I heard an old man addressing another man who was coming to meet him.

Hiya, I'm glad you're here. Haven't seen you for a while. Jesus, I was looking if I could find you on the back page of the newspaper!

Ah! No, not yet. But soon.

One of those Dublin stories. There's always a touch of acid. A taste for misfortune – not shared by everyone. It's a chronic illness. A form of atavism that I cherish. The only one, perhaps. But this one I cherish. It always squeaks where you least expect it. It's a type of laughter that smarts, that always hurts a little. A kind of jokey self-harm – you can't reinvent yourself. A few strokes with a strap, a soft one if possible, is not that unpleasant. It's a relief. Especially if you hold the strap yourself. The pleasure is proportionate to the discomfort, it intensifies as the disquiet increases. A laugh as muddy as a river bed containing as many sweet secrets stuffed into empty bottles as dead bodies that have disappeared without a trace. A laugh that contains the world and his wife and whose slim pickings is reflected in the eyes of the oldest of its inhabitants. The great old masters of laughter – which is the best thing about Ireland. We have nothing left to lose. We are impatient, even. Eager to get onto the back of the newspaper. The obituaries or the necrology section. A paper graveyard.

Deaths: So-and-so, native of Wicklow, in his 83rd year. Greatly and deservedly missed by his heartbroken wife and loving children …

It's a form of posthumous celebrity. To return to *The Third Age Gazette*. The issue I found under my door this morning is called *La Guinguette*, it refers to the ball the staff organized this summer in the garden. A Bastille Day firemen's ball relocated to the invalids' home. One can only admire the undeniably practical aspect of the event. A fireman is an old crock's ideal as he is part emergency driver, part emergency doctor. An idyllic cocktail. It was no doubt a well-run, impeccably organized ball. However, since I called in sick, I can't give a detailed account of the show. Nonetheless, as the garden is under my windows, I can testify to the choice of songs that reached my ears. Exhausting quick steps. It was as if the war had just ended. A frozen clock with broken hands. Time travel. I don't want to go back.

I imagined the stalwart sappers supporting the sad remains of flirtatious residents. Some of them are certainly all that, as the story of the little blonde old lady shows. She has lost her mind and yet, in her misfortune, has found the comfort of a tall stooped man. The one in Room 20. A handsome old man with hair and a steely gaze. He consoles her. That's something. He cuddles her, kisses her with appetite.

Embraces her like a debutante. The old blonde giggles with pleasure. Giggles with desire. Her eyes filled with wonder at her old love. Her last great love. The lover in question is as stricken as she is. In second childhood and mere oblivion. Sans teeth, sans eyes, sans taste, sans everything. A nil–all draw. Everything is wonderful. Everything would be wonderful, were it not for her dutiful husband's Sunday visits – still alive, not yet gaga. The husband witnesses the faithlessness of old age. Witnesses the love he has been unable to give to the old blonde who bubbles over and throws herself frantically into the arms of the tall, stooped man. Without even realizing it. Without any scores to settle. Shaken by a tremor more violent than the others: the thrill of last love. Not a single line about the old blonde and her tall stooped man in the *Gazette* – as the faithful readers now call it. Inane stories. Birthday photos – another year down. An extra nail in the coffin. Close-ups of lined faces, vacant eyes, bald pates crowned with pointy paper hats. Happy Birthday. A feigned deference to those who are still holding on. Fingers clutching tightly onto arthritic fingers. The only pleasure in the paper is the horoscope section. How do you say *Belier* in English again? Ah, yes, Aries. I have a faulty astrological memory.

For residents born between 21 March and 20 April: Aries
NEPTUNE IS A POSITIVE INFLUENCE: A time for reverie and introspection. Good or bad, memories will resurface, making you look to the future with wisdom. Learn from your mistakes, that is the key.
SATURN TRINE VENUS: You are loved by your loved ones faithfully and unconditionally.

PLUTO IS IN THE ASCENDANT: Be careful not to be caught by your old demons. Sarcasm. The black dog. Hidden temper tantrums. Mind your health. Don't overdo things during this difficult period.

My old demons. Have they ever let go of me? For a night? An hour? At most, they have been kept in check for a while. Tied up in the next room. Never far away. So close that I always confused them with myself. They did too, for that matter. It may well be that in the hell I don't believe in I already have a solid reputation. With my dark side rated far above average. From the head to the pelvis at least. Except the balls. You old sadist! A demon from head to toe with nothing worth saving. Have you forgotten poor Mouki, whom you threw away like an old sock? Even though you loved her. But you loved her less than you feared fear. You preferred Suzanne, who saved you a lot of trouble. Bloody balls, never there when you need them. Cowardice disguised as loyalty to the former. High-quality sadism displayed towards both. Hats off to you! No, if you count the balls and the legs that don't work any more, my dark side is so enormous that an elephant could pose his behind there. All things considered, of course.

You have made a few gestures to redeem yourself here and there. Your charity is misplaced. The prisoners didn't need you. Nor did May, who had gone mad in her hospital bed. Your mother who no longer recognized you. May was delirious, her leg hanging over that stirrup from hell. In endless agony.

And what about your brother? Your brother. There was an unfair distribution of roles – one was born to last, the other not. *Only the weed grows alone*, May said. Without food, without warmth. It grows forever. Survives storms. Survives frost. In the endless seasons in which thoughts have no rest. No respite. You are the last one on your island where the rain cries for you. Weeps horizontally. Weeps violent jets – powerful jets of sadness that wear away the rock, and sweep everything aside. Gushing up to the sky, extinguishing the stars, choking the light down to the last ray. This is your punishment. You are all alone. Good for nothing but counting corpses. Piling them under your feet. Laying flowers on the tombs you cannot visit. On which moss and lichen grow. Parasites are as immortal as the unrepentant cripple who looks at you in the mirror. You have overcome everything. You have done away with everyone. Time has made you a murderer, a matricide, a fratricide. An unfaithful widower. You have longed to be as lonely as a dog, as solitary as a wolf.

Comme un poisson hors de l'eau. Don't mix everything up – you chose your language. And so you are alone like a fish out of water. That is your inescapable fate. And here you are, suffocating far from the Irish Sea, far from the *eternal sea always lapping chattily at the end of your garden.* The sea alongside which you already wandered like a ghost when you were a child. A child already dead. Almost not born. An old man, not yet dead.

ACT THREE

'Mr Beckett? Mr Beckett, please open the door! Mr Beckett, can you hear me?'

'...'

'Quick, Françoise, help me. Mr Beckett, are you all right? Can you hear me? Squeeze my hand? It's all right. Open your eyes. That's it. Are you all right? Does anything hurt? No?'

'...'

'We'll sit you up, you'll breathe easier. Take it easy. All right, now. I'll turn your oxygen down to the minimum. Breathe easy into the mask. The doctor will be here soon.'

'...'

'Françoise, will you let them know? Dr Morin is on duty. You tell her that Mr Beckett fell out of bed. She knows him.'

'...'

'Are you all right? Are you breathing properly? That's good. You scared me! You didn't hurt yourself, did you? No? Are you sure? You can still move your limbs. Ah, you're smiling, that's a good sign. What happened to you, did you try to grab something? Did you bend over? Did you roll, is that it? Don't you know? It's not the whiskey, is it? No, it's too early. I'm teasing you, I'm teasing you. Yes, I know you are. Not a drop before 5 pm. You are very disciplined, that's good.'

'...'

'Ah, you're getting your colour back, that's better. The doctor will be here soon. I prefer to wait for him to get you up. But don't worry, I'll stay by your side. I'm not letting you out of my sight. Wait, I'll pull your vest down a bit, we can see your stomach. What do you mean? Yes, that's exactly what I mean: "*Couvrez ce sein que je ne saurais voir.*" Who is it by again? Victor Hugo? Ah, Molière?'

'...'

'I'll turn you so that you can lean back against the bed, it will be more comfortable. That's it. Is it better like that? Is the wood too hard? You tell me. You gave me a fright earlier. The beds here are high, it's quite a dive after all. What a day we've had. Madame Colard also slipped when she came out of the refectory at midday. Fortunately, nothing was broken. I hope the acrobatics are over for today. It's a good job that you're so light, if you'd been any heavier, you might have hurt yourself even more.'

'...'

*

'Mr Beckett … What's going on? Dr Morin!'

'…'

'Mr Beckett? Answer me. Can you open your eyes? Mr Beckett? Call 999, Françoise. Tell them we have a patient over eighty who has lost consciousness after falling out of bed. Nadja, did he speak to you earlier?'

'Not much, but he understood me perfectly. He just lost consciousness.'

'Pulse is stable. He's breathing. Let's put him back on the bed. Semi-upright position. Put the oxygen on low. What's his blood-pressure?'

'82/60.'

'All right, his pupils are responding, it's not a cardiac arrest. He's breathing fine. He'll come round. Let's get a line in and set up the IV. We'll give him an ECG before they get here, it'll save them some time.'

Sam has a whale of a time, as they say. A whale, that's right –
Sam is an old whale stranded on the carpet. Well a whale, in
a manner of speaking, you damned old crone. Maybe he's a
spindly specimen – a pointy-snouted finback. A particularly
self-destructive individual, who sank alone. Without any assistance from the fishermen. He drowned unexpectedly, even
though the captain was there, to the rear, ready to start the
pursuits with the harpoon between his teeth. Sam is his own
best enemy. He knows what to do. He catches himself in his
own net. A suicidal mammal. Who causes himself to fall.
Crumbles and sinks. The sea battle is over. He sailed for a
long time, old Sam. He had a good innings, when all's said
and done.

A beached whale in the deep sea – that's not a bad com-
parison. Considering I've got half my brain working too, and
not just at night. It's a permanent state. The rest is porridge.
Granny's jam. As for the whale, it keeps half a brain awake

when it sleeps. The half-brain is essential for survival, as it is designed to remind the animal of an essential crucial element – it reminds it to breathe. To come up for air regularly. A vital obligation. Which I myself too often forget. This is the proof that I overestimate myself. Do I have half a brain? A quarter, at most. Maybe less. Less than a cetacean. That's enough for what I have to do.

I wonder if I'm not mistaken. Of course, with a quarter of a brain, you can't be sure of anything. You're safe nowhere. Do whales really only think half the time? Or am I not suddenly confusing their situation with that of the dolphins? General confusion. Unrepairable noggin. Three-quarters of the way through. Come on, make an effort. Call the survivors together – I mean the few floating cells. The rare neurons that remain unharmed.

We are absolutely certain that the dolphin's brain works half the time as explained above. But what about whales? They cannot breathe at the bottom of the sea, that much is true. So they must have some trick. But that doesn't mean it's the same in each case. Do whales and dolphins have the same brain power? When I think of Melville – gosh, I can't have forgotten that. There are careful descriptions of the exceptional qualities of Moby-Dick, the whale to end all whales, and the others – high-flying cetology. Sperm whale, *Grampus*, narwhal and Moby-Dick, queen of the toothed whales. Moby-Dick was described from every angle. Moby-Dick the sperm whale – you couldn't make it up. As for the pointy-snouted finback, my brother at the bottom – at the bottom of the seabed – lurking there amongst the big family of finbacks. And not very nice, according to Melville, chief cetologist.

The Fin-Back is not gregarious. He seems a whale-hater, as some men are man-haters.

So far, it's hard to deny a certain resemblance.

Very shy; always going solitary; unexpectedly rising to the surface in the remotest and most sullen waters ...

It's getting eerie now ... The pointy-snouted finback. To be considered in case of reincarnation. Or am I already one? That would explain it.

His straight and single lofty jet rising like a tall misanthropic spear upon a barren plain ...

Melville! And his unsurpassable poetry. For the pointy-snouted finback, I understand. But I can't remember a single line about the whale's neurological activity. It must be more or less the same thing ...

Neurology Department, Hôpital Sainte-Anne

8 December 1989

'He's still sleeping, doctor. He's moaning, but he's sleeping. Do you want us to wake him up?'

'Not for the moment, the ECG results are good, he's out of danger for now. I'll come back at the end of my round. We'll see what happens between this and then. Let me know if he continues to be agitated.'

*

The title (I remember this): *Film*. Silent (me too). Black and white. (And the actors? They are there, on the tip of the tongue ...) Buster Keaton: the man. Nell Harrison and James Karen: the couple of passers-by. Susan Reed: the old lady (the famous one). A close-up on the man's eye. A ruined town (always ruins), with a huge wall covered with moss, running through it. A vertical pan of the wall, then a horizontal tracking shot to an abandoned building. A sudden movement of the camera. A view of the man running (like a horse, like a headless chicken). He stops to look at a mysterious package, with his back to the audience, then runs off again.

Keaton. Demented look. Old eyelids wrinkled like prunes. Like an old bag. A colourless gaze devouring the screen with its iris and which, rather than acting like a veil, was more like a trap door, *a back door* that was hidden in the wallpaper, perfectly embedded in the pattern, covering unmentionable things. Under everyone's nose. Unmentionable things – which ones? I didn't know. I was looking for them when I made *Film*. I filmed and scrapped things. No matter how hard I tried to pierce it, not the eye itself, but its secret, nothing filtered through. Nothing other than the mad authority of this eye inhabited the screen. It took it all in. Every corner. Keaton occupied the set and drew it to him like a magnet. A hard magnetic material with a strong remanent magnetization and a coercive field. A disturbingly attractive force, even for me on the other side. The eye – mine this time – glued to the viewfinder, in the small window from which I was trying to make a frame. An eye for an eye – let's leave out the teeth, mine riveted to Keaton's, which was absorbing everything, like a sponge. Yes, that's right, like a sponge, whose eyeholes, like miniature vases, were ready to collect anything that wanted to be poured into them. He had a spongy eye. Not really an eye. Not like the others. It was particularly moist. No outpouring though. An eye studded with red protruding veins, moist as if it were preparing to send a rain shower on anyone who looked at it the wrong way. If it contained tears, they were those of its victims. Some unlucky people who one day, maybe one evening, had crossed its path without really paying it any attention. Just a glance, in passing. It had cost them dearly. They had never come back from it. Like a spider, the eye had spun its web until it attracted them. Until it held them. So as to absorb their tears. It suffered from great dryness. Not a drop left. An ocular vampire. A bottomless eye like a blind pupil. The pupil of a blind man who sees. An abominable pupil. The eye of a Cyclops that has two. The last straw.

In his rush, the man bumps into a couple of passers-by reading a newspaper (well, reading – looking at the headlines). A quick shot of the passer-by who wobbles, then catches himself. A close-up on the passer-by who looks at the man, intrigued. The man slips between them and resumes his run. He straddles the rubble and walks on the planks. The camera returns to the passer-by who puts his hat and glasses back on (that's it, they've seen him. He's in danger). A close-up of the passers-by side by side staring at the camera and shouting.

They saw me too. They saw my eye in the viewfinder. You thought you were safe behind your little window. You thought you were calculating the angles and they didn't notice. Your eye was trapped. It too was trapped in the film. The Cyclops is you, old man. The monster – son of Ouranos and Gaia. But which one? Brontes, Steropes, or Ares?

No, not at all, nothing to do with the Cyclops. You are only one eye among the others. Besides, they too have been seen, I mean by people other than you. Even the man could not escape. Despite the thousand and one precautions he took to blend in with the background. Nothing could be done. Despite the black cloak that enveloped his figure. In spite of the hat he stuck on his head that was itself covered with a silky fabric like a suit pocket. A cloth that he had taken care to tuck under his boater to hide his face better. He was seen, too. Maybe not identified, but who knows? And what if his photo was in the newspaper, in the newspaper the pass-er-by was holding? His photo was printed, a close-up, on the news page. Ah, he can run like a rabbit, like a bat out of hell who flaps its wings to blind the raptor, its predator. In this case it transforms him into a rat. Caught red-handed in his mad rush. Photographed in full flight.

*

'The cardiac tests are good, it seems. There's no reason why he shouldn't come to. Have you tried to wake him up?'

'Not yet, we were waiting for you, Doctor. He's still very agitated but he's keeping his eyes closed. It's like he's having a nightmare.'

'Mr Beckett? Mr Beckett, can you hear me? Open your eyes if you can. I see your eyelids moving. You can open them. Go ahead and try.'

'...'

'Can you see me? I'm Dr Utrillo. You are in hospital. No, no, keep your eyes open. I know it's tiring but you'll get used to it. Sorry about the little light in your eye, I'm just quickly checking your pupils. That's fine. Follow my finger. That's fine.'

'...'

'Do you remember what happened? You can take the mask off if it makes it hard to talk. Do you remember? You fainted at the nursing home. You fell out of bed. And as we don't know the exact reason we're going to run some additional tests. Your family is on the way, your nephews, I think. They are from Ireland, right?'

'...'

'Well, don't tire yourself out too much, but try to stay awake a bit. We'll bring you some food. I'll come back and see you later. No, no, don't go back to sleep just yet. Try to keep your eyes open as much as possible. See you later, Mr Beckett.'

*

Travelling on the man who turns the corner (at full speed, always at full speed) and enters a building. Zoom in on the man who stops and puts his fingers on his wrist to check his pulse (one hundred beats per minute, at the very least).

How old might Keaton have been at the time of the film? Seventy? Seventy-five? No idea. Not a newcomer, anyway. Although he was still hopping round like a scalded cat, the old acrobat. He'd already had a few falls, as demonstrated by his build, which had been so graceful and has become stout. Not fat, no. Not a beer belly, but still, not a skinnymalink. Still, I thought to myself, seeing him in such good shape, the grey-haired guy would certainly be out of breath after such a race. Hence my idea that he should stop for a moment to take his pulse. And check that the machine was in working order. Talk about a buffalo! Keaton was still a funny guy, a kid compared to the piece of junk you are now. Look at this old crock criticizing him, when my life is already three-quarters of the way through. And that's a rough fraction. What remains of the Sam who followed the camera, climbed the ladder into the clouds? A vegetable. A floppy carrot or parsnip smelling of camphor and mould.

*

'*Houhou, Monsieur?*'

'…'

'Good morning. Sorry, I was asked to wake you up. I'll bring you your tray. Be careful, it's very hot. I will remove the lids and open the pots for you.'

'…'

'So, today, you have mushroom soup as a starter. For the main course, the staff who look after you at Le Tiers-Temps explained to us that you don't eat meat, so I've replaced the ham and butter beans with a medallion of hake and rata-touille, I hope that's OK. Do you like fish?'

'…'

'A little bit of Vicq cheese? I'll spread it on your bread, it will be easier to eat. And for dessert, a Flanby, that will go down fine. You're making a face. Don't you like blancmange? That's okay, I can get you stewed fruit if you prefer. Apple or rhubarb?'

'…'

*

The travelling goes up and down on the man who climbs a few steps, sees an old lady (she's really old, in fact. No debate) and goes back down to hide under the stairwell. She hasn't seen him, she continues down the stairs with a basket of flowers in her hand. Close-up on the old lady's face. Her smile fades. A look of terror. Her eyes bulge out. She collapses. The flowers scatter on the ground. Vertical travelling. The man was behind her, he fled upstairs.

This time we get it. Of course, it is a more than clear-cut trick. However, he was so sly that he managed to escape once again. I mean to escape the eye – mine, the camera's – which did not catch him. It allowed him to leg it. He won't take his geronto-phobic crime with him to heaven. The poor old woman was pushed down the stairs with a sharp shove. Nothing could be easier. No need for much. She was hanging on by a thread for ages. Hanging on by a thread. Just one, which he broke off like one of the Fates. With a short sharp movement – you'd think it was an accident. The old woman fell down the steps. The elegant old woman, with her black doll's eyes and her flowery hat. Real flowers, which the coquette had carefully tied onto the front of the hat. A white rose and a thistle. Now in a heap next to the old woman. Next to the dead woman.

Can you see that the old woman meant so much more to him? It was probably his mother! If not, why did he do that? Why else would he push her? It wouldn't make sense. Neither head nor tail to it. It was her, the old woman with eyes as black as holes, who was mainly responsible. She was the one responsible for his existence. Guilty of everything. She had hidden her cruelty behind a mask for such a long time. Behind her flowery hat. She was a succubus. A seductive demon, punishing men for their treachery. Of course, they are all traitors! You above all. There is no need to look very far. The corpses are all there, cursed skeletons lurking in the back of the cupboards, just waiting to come out. No, the old woman deserved her pitiful end – one final inaudible cry, and the silent film transmits only the image.

Neurology Department, Hôpital Sainte-Anne

9 December 1989

'Hello sir, I've come to … Mr Beckett?'

'…'

'Were you sleeping? I'm sorry to bother you, I've come to wash you. My colleagues told me that you asked for a man to wash you. My name is Frederic.'

'…'

'So that I don't tire you too much, I'll give you a quick wash in bed. Wait, I'll put on my apron and I'll go and fill the bowl next to us. I'll be right back. Do you prefer a shower mitt or a sponge?'

'…'

'It's not too hot, is it? Does it feel good? I'll shave you tomorrow, if you like. There, we're done the top part; now for the armpits, watch out, I'll try not to tickle you too much. What did you say?'

'...'

'Wait, I'm changing the mitt. Sorry, but I have to wash you all over. Here too. I'll hurry up, I'll do it quickly.'

'...'

'That's it, the hardest part's done. You can pull down your shirt, I don't mind doing the legs and feet.'

'...'

'There you go, clean as a new penny. What did you say? *Clean as a whistle*? Ah, that's nice, I didn't know that expression.'

*

Close-up on the man's hands opening a lock. He enters the room, closes the door and puts the chain to lock himself in. He takes his pulse again (incurable hypochondriac).

Back to the room. The one from childhood. The one in which he begged at night for a lamp to be turned on to quench his fear. The familiar, strange room, with walls that are cracked like a skin revealing veins. Leaving the sorrows visible. A thin skin, a fragile envelope – not really protective. Familiar in spite of everything. Like an old ache. The man can finally remove the cloth that hid his face. He is finally safe.

You can see nothing! You never see any of the details of the surroundings. You forget about the window, through which a view from the busy street alone could give him away. In spite of the curtains with which the man struggles and which, with their endless holes, leave him exposed. They expose him to the scaffold – he will not escape the crime of matricide. He knows it. Or only if fortune favours him. And why shouldn't it favour him? It favoured you. Favoured you most favourably. And you didn't get caught. The others did. They were swept away. You were lucky. You were making hay while the sun shone. They got caught. Now it's his turn. The man knows it.

Panoramic shot of the room: we see a sideboard with a cage and an aquarium on it. Quick camera movement showing a rocking chair, a poster (perhaps a portrait of Punch, I mean the puppet) and a mirror hanging on the wall. Close-up on the centre of the room where there is a basket, in which a small-breed dog and a black-and-white cat are lying.

I said safe. Not out of sight. If the man was out of sight, there would be no film. Here he is, safe, with animals for companions. He should be happy – he is a misanthropist, a wild thing. He likes no one but beasts. Beasts are fun. Especially in the countryside, it's true. Still, they seem surprisingly quiet for animals that have been left indoors for a while. The cat and the dog are usually always up for a walk – on the road again. There was no fuss. Barely a blink of an eye. They are waiting, curled up in their baskets. There are other ways to skin a cat. And a dog.

You're still being played like a rookie. By the kitty basket cat and the doggy basket. The man understood that right away. He sensed the danger. The looks are programmed like grenades. Like bombs. He felt them coming at him each one in turn. Even those that were surreptitiously hiding in the cracks or in the reflections of the mirror. He felt them all. First the parrot, then the cat and finally the Chihuahua … There was nothing he could do but kick them out! Get the fuck outta here!

Wide shot on the room – the man takes the cat in his arms, opens the door, puts the cat outside, closes the door. Pan right – the man picks up the dog, opens door, kicks the dog out. The cat takes the opportunity to come back inside.

One goes out, the other comes in. It's an old gag. A comedy trick, which still makes me laugh. Almost as much as the other old chestnut, *Hold on to the brush, I'm taking down the ladder.* It's still the best of all. I hear there's even a theological version. The devil still laughs at it, so he does.

What happens next? What happens once the ladder is removed? What else can happen? Nothing. Nothing ever happens. Nothing good ever happens when you are alone, in the dark in a room and the light, the simple light of day, is enough to reveal the crime and its culprit. The matricide. What do you want the matricide to do? Apart from hiding, apart from hating himself. Apart from running away from his own reflection. *Self-hatred* is the term in English. It doesn't matter, you idiot, because the film is silent. Since everyone hates themselves, at one point or another. Especially at the end. When the wreckage of the body is matched only by the wreckage of the mind, which is falling apart. And the accusatory voices grow louder. Even when you can't hear them.

Neurology Department, Hôpital Sainte-Anne

10 December 1989

'Mr Beckett?'

'...'

'As you can see, Madame Fournier, Mr Beckett is very tired, he sleeps a lot these days. We have to wake him up for his treatment and his meals.'

'...'

'Mr Beckett? It's the doctor. Please open your eyes, I'd like to talk to you.'

'...'

'As I was explaining to your friend Madame Fournier, the results of the examinations have unfortunately not given us that much insight into your situation. We don't know the cause of the syncopes. And so, for the moment, we are continuing with the treatment and monitoring his situation carefully.'

'...'

'Well, I'll leave you to it. I think you're going to get some reading done, Mr Beckett. It's good to have some stimulation. What's that? William Butler Yeats? I don't know him. Is he Irish?'

*

Horizontal panning: the blanket falls off the mirror, the man throws himself on it and covers it up again. Circular camera movements. The man sits on the rocking chair and picks up the package he was carrying earlier. At the start of the film.

I liked the idea of loot. The idea of a little stash that Keaton had carried from God knows where. I liked it. Not the Harpagon tape, nor the gangster-style briefcase of cash. No, a rather modest booty. A booty that would only be a booty for him, in the end. That had a sentimental value. Now that he's standing there like a pirate in the room, his patch pulled down over his eye. Now that he has cleared his mind, now that he is settled in the armchair. He'll finally be able to open it, the mysterious package from the leather briefcase, which is none other than ...

Shut up! You always have to go too fast. Much too fast. You want to tell things before they happen. Damned Pythia! Rotten Pythoness! A snake, that's what you are. A filthy reptile living in a cave, terrorizing his comrades. You speak of an oracle, at this stage we still know nothing of what is in the briefcase. We only know that the man attaches extraordinary importance to it. That he holds it close to his heart like a woman. As if his existence depended on it. He would rather die than lose it. Than lose it like you lost your wife.

Close-up of the parrot in the cage. Camera behind the man walking towards the cage and taking off his cloak. Close-up of the parrot's eye winking. Camera behind the man covering the cage with his cape. Close-up of the aquarium and the goldfish. Camera behind the man walking towards the aquarium and covering it too.

Of course, one always thinks of the voyeur's pleasure – a real pleasure, I know what I'm talking about. But what about the other person's displeasure? Scopophobia. I mean the one who is being observed and fears the pleasure of the voyeur. Fears it as one fears shame. As one fears punishment. Enjoyment taken, in a way, without his consent.

Finally, when I say enjoyment, I mean enjoyment in the broad sense. I'm not thinking of sex, in this case, nor of Keaton for that matter. I even carefully avoid thinking about the two at the same time. Wrong mix, as far as I'm concerned. Ah, tastes and colours. Keaton, what I wanted was to see him. Behind my viewfinder. Not only to see him seeing, but also to see him being seen. Or imagining he was being seen. I wondered how long he would last. How high the tension would go. The tension that was rising within him like milk in a pan on the flame at full blast. I could feel his delirium growing as if it were inside me. I was happy it was happening to someone else, glad that it had chosen another. Glad it had chosen Keaton. Keaton's your man.

Here he is, confessing, the barbaric screenwriter, the diabolical director. A torturer, no better. He fed the evil. First the window, then the mirror and even the horrible goldfish with eyes like globes. Now that he has covered them with his cloak, perhaps he will finally be able to breathe. And open the mysterious briefcase.

Camera behind the man rocking in the chair. Zoom in on the briefcase he opens and from which he takes out pictures.
Photo number 1 and 2: Portraits of a woman wearing a hat.
Photo number 3: A dandy and a dog showing off in front of him on a table.

But who is this beautiful elegant severe-looking woman? Where the hell did this picture come from? From an abandoned corner of the brain. Goldfish memory. More holes than Swiss cheese. A memory in tatters that shakes the images like snowflakes in a snow globe.

Who is this woman? With her old-fashioned cape. His wife? His mother, when she was young, before he was born? Before he was born and she went completely crazy. She was already a little crazy. She had always been. A madwoman in the making. Not yet complete. Not yet his mother.

The mother, the mother! Stop it with the mother! All you think about is her, even though she's dead and buried in Greystones. Between the sea and the mountains. The mountains of Wicklow. That's not her. She's not in the film. Not in the briefcase. Not even in this picture. Besides, the man isn't even looking at her any more, he's moved on to the next picture. The picture of the dandy.

A dandy with a hat, cane and moustache, a touch of affectation in his manner – a cliché. He bows to a dog, which is itself perched on a table. The dog is also showing off – on its hind legs, stretched out towards its master. Feigned deference; the dandy hides a sugar lump in his sleeve.

Look closely. Doesn't this dandy leaning over his dog remind you of someone? You can't have forgotten! Not him. Look again: the striped suit, the cane, the moustache ... Don't you recognize the master, poor dog?

No, I'm positive about that. Joyce was thinner. Much thinner. He looked like a beanpole with his big sticks, I mean his legs, and his pointy chin. Pointed like a beak. Like a nail.

The nails you're talking about are the ones in his coffin! Joyce is dead. Remember that. You always forget. He died in the war, there's nothing left of him. There wasn't even enough left of him, not enough of his remains to bring back to Ireland. You tried, but it was no use. Joyce had turned to dust.

Yes, Joyce is dead. The war was the end of him. The end of the master, dead among the dead. Died a death that had nothing to do with it. Nothing to do with the war. Yet ... Yet Joyce's words are there, unharmed in my worn cortex. Words miraculously rescued from all the shipwrecks. From all my shipwrecks. They are there, always ready to come out. They lead me inexorably back to this girl, this mountain flower. Words of honey. Joyce's words don't bang. Don't jerk. Don't hammer. They chirp like the thrush that came to me from the mountains. The thrush that I used to see coming in the distance from the kitchen window, in the mornings in Foxrock, at the hour when the souls in the house were already preoccupied by daylight. When I stood there in May's kitchen, watching the thrush in the distance show me the way. The path of freedom that runs through the sky. From the sea to the mountains. Overlooking everything. I was wrecked on the rocks with Joyce's words in my head. Joyce's words in my heart. In chorus, chirping their story of girl, of mountain flower – tweet, tweet. Here they are tweeting again even as night lurks. They take up the story for me – my memory is walking memory, my memory is flying. I am listening.

Yes, the girl, like all Andalusian girls, put a rose in her hair. A red rose. There was also the story of the wall and the kiss. Of a girl who, considering that fellow one was no worse than any other, perhaps slightly above average, had finally taken the plunge. Yes, Joyce's indelible yesses jostle each other. Another yes. Repeated desire. A yes planted straight in the eyes – a form of universal language. It does not mean 'yes', it means 'again'. She says again. Yes again for the embrace and for the racing heart and yes I said yes I will Yes.

Photo number 4: A student in formal wear receiving his diploma from his teacher.

The laureate's mortarboard with its beloved tassel – a university in the anglophone world. Yes, but which one? No conclusive clues. Is the man, the killer, a Trinity College alumnus who later opted to go down the wrong road? Could he be one of those lost sheep of which the good shepherd speaks? A parable of the good shepherd who met the wrong people. Those bad companions we were told about in church on Sundays while I was dozing in my chair?

Unless it wasn't him. Look closely. That's not the man in the picture. Look at that long lanky fellow. That long-haired fellow with the long hair under the cap. You can see that it's you! You, always you, the swot with the round glasses, proud as a god, rising up like a mountain, proud to appear in that get-up in front of your teachers. In front of your parents.

*

'You can talk to him. Your uncle can hear you. He is very agitated, for the reasons I explained to you, nevertheless, when he opens his eyes and comes to, most of the time he is coherent. I would advise you to speak to him in English, perhaps that can create some extra stimulation. We don't know. It's worth a try. Shall I come and see him again tomorrow? We'll review the situation together, if you like.'

*

Photo number 5: Wedding photo. A couple poses in front of a garden gate.

We know what awaits them, the poor unfortunates. Both buried up to the waist. He is sleeping. She is half-mad. Alone, next to each other. With only the little things on the horizon, the tiny gestures that keep them away from the end. Brushing their teeth at set times and talking about nothing. Modest pleasures. Brushing time. In the photo, they do not yet know what awaits them. In the photo, the couple is elegant, but modest. The groom wears a simple jacket. No morning suit, no waistcoat tied in the back, no blue mohair overcoat. And definitely no stiff-collared shirt.

Why would the groom need all that? Those outfits only exist in stories. Stories of others that your memory regurgitates.

For a wedding, a simple jacket is enough. The jacket is not going to make a difference.

Yes, I agree, the jacket is enough. It may even be too much, given the difficult circumstances, the marital ordeal – an oxymoron – that awaits them. We all have to deal with it. That's why I didn't wear one on my wedding day. My wedding day. I could never bring myself to use this word to describe my affair – in this case there is none, by chance of the sentence – with Suzanne. It seems so inappropriate to me. I mean marriage. Well, inappropriate, let's say that what bothers me is the gap – decidedly, the gap between marriage as we usually understand it and marriage as it absorbs us. As it digests us and finally rejects us. It rejects itself, like a bad transplant. There is never any information on this subject in the news. No warning about this scourge, which has been claiming countless victims for thousands of years. Not a single word until you are confronted with it yourself. Before it is too late. Even though we are fed a daily diet of the price of a barrel of oil – around nineteen dollars, I believe? Never mind. The fact remains that on my wedding day, I didn't wear a jacket. Only my old sheepskin jacket and my beret. And I put up with it, my warm old skin, on that freezing day. I put up with it, just as Suzanne put up with the fur she was wrapped up in, with a hood on her head. Not beauty and the beast but almost – we were so old, Suzanne and I, we were so cold. Old people playing at being husbands and wives. Scarecrows. Scary. The inside of her hood was also stuffed with her few white locks that were sticking out. The locks of her famous bob – for that was her hairstyle. A medium-length bob with a thick fringe covering her mathematician's forehead. That's what they say,

162

she had a mathematician's forehead. She wasn't one, though. Suzanne was a piano player. It was always the piano. The rest was just rubbish to her. Leftovers from the day before.

Photo number 6: Photo taken in a garden in front of a house. A man is holding a child in his arms.

The eternal baby in the photo. Taken when he was still a baby. In his father's arms. It didn't last long. A year or two at the most. Time is flying. Time flew by like the wind, taking its share of dust with it. The dust of childhood.

We think it is flying, but it's never-ending. How much longer will all this go on for? Nobody knows. You wouldn't have bet much on your own duration. Yet on you go. Despite everything. Despite your wounds. Despite the war. Despite your legs. While the others, all the others who were so strong, lay down with their mouths open. Your mouth is still moaning. Only good for belching out bad thoughts. Absurd memories. The hero of the film got rid of them. He tore up the photos with his big paws. In one swift movement. The fragments of glossy paper multiplied under his murderous hands. Painful pieces. Eliminated one after the other. Paper murderer. First the child, who did not remain a child. Then the wife. Now he's going backwards again. Until the graduation ceremony. What will be left in the end? Is there anything left at all? Even the dog. Even Joyce. Confetti.

Neurology Department, Hôpital Sainte-Anne

11 December 1989

'I'm sorry to have to tell you that Mr Beckett didn't wake up this morning.'

[A pause]

'He had another syncope during the night. He entered a state that I would describe as a Level 2 coma. This means that his ability to wake up has gone. We can't really reach him any more, even if he can possibly hear us, I can't answer that, we don't really know.'

[A pause]

'On the other hand, he still reacts to painful stimuli. He is still very agitated. I will give you precise information this afternoon on the protocol that the team has come up with in order to make him as comfortable as possible.'

'Of course, we won't do anything without your agreement. In the absence of a son or daughter, you are the closest
members of his family. So you are the decision-makers. I don't
know if he had outlined his wishes regarding his medical care.
If you don't mind, we will resume this discussion later on. I will
let you spend some time with him. I'll see you this afternoon.'

*

I'm willing to make a clean sweep. Let's tear up the photos and
the rest. Off you hop, into the bin. Good riddance. *Bébé jeté
avec l'eau du bain* – baby thrown out with the bathwater – for
once we agree in both languages. For once we are saying the
same thing. Last-minute synchronization. Could it be a sign?
A sign of what? The whole shebang? The child sacrificed, like
the lamb. After all, it wouldn't be the first time. And then,
what does it change? None of this can change. The man may
sit there in his rocking chair, he may have crushed the images
with his hands, but they remain there. Scattered. Sticking to
his heels. The images of the living dead, photographed before
they were. Frozen in the happiness that precedes the grave.
And you. You were born at the edge, at the very edge of the
cliff, you miraculously followed its peak. You felt the crumbly
rock under your feet. You could feel the rockslides as you
passed. You could hardly see anything in the thick fog. In the
fog of war. You could not see, yet you could hear the cries of
those who were falling. Or of those who had already fallen
and were still waiting to succumb to their open wounds.

It lasted a long time. An eternity of hearing the cries of others. A show in three acts. With an intermission. There were always intermissions. Cursed jolts. Final reflexes. It was already over. All puppets disarticulated by the fall. Broken bones, going in all directions. Coming out of the reddened flesh that pissed like lava. Comrades tortured to the bone. Picking up coal with their bare hands. Not even strong enough to lift a shovel.

You always exaggerate. That was during the war. It wasn't always like this. Others knew the sweetness of home. Death at home. Loved ones around. The patient dressed and undressed by familiar hands. The privilege of the parent. Of the one who begot. Of the one who gave birth.

What do you know about it? What do you know about the body of the parents delivered to the hands of their offspring, you who did not have any? You who never wanted one.

Obviously, there is still some doubt. Even in my old age. Doubt disguised as hope. A lost son, found. No, better, a daughter. Yes, a daughter. Daughter of a love I would have let run away. That I would have allowed to disappear. An American girl of thirty-two, as beautiful as a lit-up picture. As precious as the treasures swallowed by the ocean I allowed to separate us. One more time. One last time. This time was the one. This time it was the end. Mouki disappeared. Well, almost. A few more letters. Just letters. No son. No daughter. Useless regrets.

You do know that people's descendants are cruel, don't you? That they take over the familiar body of the sick, the father or the mother, and they suffocate it? Or, worse, they dream of doing so? You yourself have thought of this so often. You have thought of shortening the lives of your sick family members. Convinced that you would do them good.

Desperate to satisfy the deep hatred that has always been in you and that their death has relieved. Admit it. You were relieved to see them go. The sadness was less intense than the relief caused by death. By the deaths you witnessed. You were satisfied like the murderer who watches the final scene and watches the poison do its work. The poison you were preparing all your life. Fuelled by your hatred, embellished with your bile, that suddenly got what it wanted. To your shame you wanted their end. The others were your poison.

*

'Please, take a seat. I will answer all your questions. We need to come to an agreement and you need to understand the protocol that we are putting in place to help your uncle.

'First, with regard to sedation. There are three main indicators for sedation: delirium, or agitation if you prefer, dyspnoea, difficulty in breathing, pain, of course, and more rarely vomiting.

'In this case, it is mainly the agitation that prompts me to suggest sedation. I think we can do something about the constant state of anxiety that Mr Beckett has been in for the last few days and which became much worse last night.

'I should explain that there are several levels of sedation. In order to relieve your uncle, we will have to put him into a deep coma. Our goal, since we can't do anything else for him, is to make him as comfortable as possible.

'Do we have your consent for morphine?

'Have you other questions?'

What's the point of telling you about what happened at the end? There is nothing to tell. What happened always happened before. Long before. Or just before. But always before. Nobody knows what happens at the end. Before the end, there's nothing to be seen. There's nothing to see.

Just before the end of *Film*, a man rocks back and forth in a rocking chair made of dark wood. He rocks to soothe himself as if he were in the arms of his nanny. If he were in her arms she would sing to him. Nanny sings. *Hush little baby*. Nanny sings and promises the moon. Promises of dawn.

> Hush little baby, don't say a word
> Mama's going to buy you a mockingbird

Each word brings its share of promises. A nanny promises everything. A whole lot of presents that will buy a baby's silence. But a child cries, he can't help himself. What else can he do now that he knows, now that we all know the sun is setting and night is falling. A never-ending movement. It happens this way every day. The child knows it. Each day holds the promise of a return of the light, which then fades away, inexorably. It slips away. An ephemeral light is blown out each evening. Midnight. The light is quenched. Morning is still so far off. Unattainable happiness. Waiting? Waiting – that is always the problem. Waiting, what to do when waiting? Cry out. Why not? There's nothing like cries to scare the shadows. To keep the wolves at bay since the fire has gone out. Nothing to hang on to, just your own voice bleating – a reassuring presence. An Irish nanny might sing in her native tongue, *Seoithín, seo hó*.

> *Seoithín a leanbh is codail go fóill*
> (Hush baby sleep a while)
>
> *Ar mhulach an tí tá síoda geala*
> (On the roof of the house there are white fairies)
>
> *Faoi chaoin ré an Earra ag imirt is spoirt*
> (Who frolic and sport under the spring moon)
>
> *Seo iad aniar iad le glaoch ar mo leanbh*
> (Here they come, calling my baby)
>
> *Le mian é tharraingt san lios mór*
> (Taking him away to their great fairy fort)

She can threaten him all she likes. The fairies cannot compare with the peril that night holds in store. The dark side from which no one escapes. The side of the half-empty glass.

So, why don't you cry out?

Try, damn it, try! Go on, show your mettle. Rage, dear old Sam, in any language you like! Yell, you fiend, like a drill sergeant! Like a banshee! Warn people of the dangers, of the dark. Of the night. Sound the warning bell. Yell like a banshee, tell them another death is coming. Death is approaching. Yell, if you still can.

Samuel Beckett really existed and he did end his days in a retirement home called Le Tiers-Temps in Paris, where he had been living in exile for half a century. Yet this book is a novel. My undertaking is not biographical. It reconstructs a version of Beckett from real and imaginary facts, as if he were a character at the end of his life, like those who inhabit his own work.